I0587756

Dead
in the
Water

A Provincetown Mystery

Jeannette de Beauvoir

HOMEPORT
P R E S S

Dead in the Water: A Provincetown Mystery
Copyright © 2020 by Jeannette de Beauvoir

Published by HomePort Press
PO Box 1508
Provincetown, MA 02657
www.HomePortPress.com

ISBN   978-1-7340533-7-1
eISBN 978-1-7340533-8-8

Cover Design by Miladinka Milic

Dead in the Water is a work of fiction. Other than those individuals who have given their permission and certain well-known landmarks, all names, characters, places, situations, and incidents are the products of the author's imagination and used fictitiously. Any other resemblance to actual events, or persons, living or dead, is purely coincidental.

Also by
Jeannette de Beauvoir

Mysteries:
Sydney Riley series:
> *Death of. Bear*
> *Murder at Fantasia Fair*
> *The Deadliest Blessing*
> *A Killer Carnival*
> *A Fatal Folly*
> *The Matinée Murders*
> *The Lethal Legacy*

Martine LeDuc series:
> *Deadly Jewels*
> *Asylum*

Trinity Pierce series:
> *Murder Most Academic* (as Alicia Stone)

Historical Fiction:
Our Lady of the Dunes
Lethal Alliances

1

It was, I told myself, all my worst nightmares come true. All at once.

I may live at Land's End, out at the tip of Cape Cod where the land curls into itself and for centuries foghorns warned of early death and disaster; I may have, yes, been out on boats on the Atlantic waters, laughably close to shore; but no, I'd never gotten used to any of it. I like floors that don't move under my feet. I like knowing I could conceivably make it back to land on my own steam should something go wrong. (Well the last bit is a fantasy: without a wetsuit, the cold would get me before the fatigue did. But the point still stands.)

I was having this plethora of cheerful thoughts for two reasons. I had allowed myself to be persuaded to go on a whale watch.

And the person standing beside me on the deck was my mother.

Like all stories that involve me and my mother, this one started with guilt. I'd had, safe to say, a rough year. I'd broken my arm (and been nearly killed) at an extremely memorable film festival here in Provincetown in the spring, and then during Women's Week that October had met up with another murderer—seriously, it's as if my friend Julie Agassi, the head of the town's police detective squad, is right, and I go looking for these things.

I don't, but people are starting to wonder.

Meanwhile, my mother was busily beating her you-never-call-you-never-write drum and I just couldn't face seeing her for the holidays. My life was already complicated enough, and there's no one like my mother for complicating things further. She's in a class by herself. Other contenders have tried valiantly to keep up, before falling, one by one, by the wayside. Not even death or divorce can complicate my life the way my mother manages to. She *perseveres*.

On the other hand, circumstances had over the past year given her a run for her money. My boyfriend Ali—who after several years my mother continued to refer to as *that man*—and I had become sudden and accidental godparents to a little girl named Lily when our friend Mirela adopted her sister's unwanted baby. And the godparents thing—which I'd always assumed to be a sort of ceremonial role one trotted out at Christmas and birthdays—had become very real when Mirela was arrested, incarcerated, and investigated as to her parenting suitability last October, and suddenly we were *in loco parentis.* I took the baby to Ali's Boston apartment and we holed up there for over a month. Mirela had joined us for the last week of it and I can honestly say I've never been more relieved to see anyone in my life.

I was trying, but motherhood was clearly not my gig. Maybe there's something to that DNA thing, after all.

What with one thing and another, it was this January before I was thinking straight. I'd gone back to my life in P'town and my work—I'm the wedding and events planner for the Race Point Inn, one of the town's nicer establishments, though I do say it myself—and really believed I was finally feeling back to what passes for normal again when my mother began her barrage of guilt-laden demands. Had I forgotten I had parents? I could travel to Boston, but not to New Hampshire?

It hadn't helped that, because there was absolutely nothing on the inn's events calendar for February, Ali and I decided to be the tourists for once; we'd taken off for Italy. Okay, let's see, the short dark days of February... and a choice between snowy New Hampshire and the charms of Venice. You tell me.

Which was why I'd run out of excuses by the time my mother started taking about being on her deathbed in March. (She wasn't.) And that my father had forgotten what I looked like in April. (He hadn't.)

I couldn't afford any more time off—Glenn, the inn's owner, had already been more than generous as it was—and there was only one thing to do. I had a quick shot of Jameson's for courage and actually called my mother, risking giving her a heart attack (the last time I'd called was roughly two administrations ago), and invited her and my father to come to Provincetown.

Which was why I now found myself on the deck of the Dolphin IV, looking for whales and listening to my mother read from the guidebook. "The largest living mammal is the blue whale," she reported.

"I know," I acknowledged.

"The humpback whale doesn't actually chew its food," she said. "It filters it through baleens."

"I know," I replied.

She glanced at me, suspicious. "How do *you* know all this?"

"Ma, I live in Provincetown." It's just possible one or two of the year-round residents—there aren't that many of us, the number is under three thousand—don't know about whales, but the possibility is pretty remote. Tourism is our only real industry. Tourists stop us in the street to ask us questions.

We know about whales.

She sniffed. "You don't have to take an attitude about it, Sydney Riley," she said. Oh, good: we were in full complete-name reprimand mode. "You know I don't like it when you take an attitude with me."

"I wasn't taking an attitude. I was stating a fact." I could feel the slow boil of adolescent-level resentment—and attitude, yes—building. I am in my late thirties, and I can still feel about fifteen when I'm having a conversation with my mother. *Breathe, Riley,* I counseled myself. *Just breathe. Deeply. Don't let her get to you.*

She looked around her. "Are we going to see sharks?"

I sighed. Everyone these days wants to see sharks. For a long time, the dreaded story of *Jaws* was just that—a story, something to watch at the drive-in movie theatre in Wellfleet (yeah, we still have one of those) and shiver deliciously at the creepy music and

5

scream when the shark tries to eat the boat. But conservation efforts over the past eight or ten years had caused a spectacular swelling of the seal population around the Cape—we'd already seen a herd of them sunning themselves on the beach today when we'd passed Long Point—and a few years later, the Great White sharks realized where their meals had all gone, and followed suit.

That changed things rather a lot. A tourist was attacked at a Truro beach and bled out. Signs were posted everywhere. Half-eaten seal corpses washed up. The famous annual Swim for Life, which once went clear across the harbor, changed its trajectory. And everybody downloaded the Great White Shark Conservancy's shark-location app, Sharktivity.

The reality is both scary and not-scary. We'd all been surprised to learn sharks are quite comfortable in three or four feet of water, so merely splashing in the shallows was out. But in reality sharks attack humans only when they mistake them for seals, and usually only bite once, as our taste is apparently offensive to them. People who die from a shark attack bleed out; they're not eaten alive.

"We might," I said to my mother now. "There are lots of kinds of sharks here—"

The naturalist's voice came over the loudspeaker, saving me. "Ah, so the captain tells me we've got a female and her calf just up ahead, at about two o'clock off the bow of the boat."

"What does that mean, two o'clock?"

He had already told us. My mother had been asking what they put in the hot dogs in the galley at the time and hadn't stopped to listen to him. "If the front of the boat is twelve o'clock, then two o'clock is just off—there!" I exclaimed, carried away despite myself. "There! Ma, see?"

"What?"

The whale surfaced gracefully, water running off her back, bright and sparkling in the sunlight, and just as gracefully went back under. A smaller back followed suit. The denizens of the deep, here to feed for the summer, willing to show off for the boatloads of visitors who populated the whale-watch fleet every year to catch a glimpse of another life, a mysterious life echoing with otherworldly calls and harkening back to times when the oceans were filled with giants.

Before we hunted them to the brink of extinction, that is.

"This is an individual we know," the naturalist was saying. "Her name is Perseid. Unlike some other whales, humpbacks don't travel in pods. Instead, they exist in loose and temporary groups that shift, with individuals moving from group to group, sometimes swimming on their own. These assemblages have been referred to as fluid fission/fusion groups. The only exception to this fluidity is the cow and calf pair. This calf was born eight months ago, and while right now you're seeing her next to Perseid, she's going to start straying farther and farther away as the summer progresses."

Now that my mother was quieter—even she was silent in the face of something this big, this extraordinary—I recognized the naturalist's voice. It was Kai Bennett, who worked at the Center for Coastal Studies in town; he was a regular at the Race Point Inn's bar scene during the winter, when we ran a trivia game and he aced all the biology questions. "And we have another one that just went right under us... haven't yet seen who this one is," said Kai.

The newcomer spouted right off the port side of the boat and the light wind swept a spray of fine droplets over the passengers, who exclaimed and laughed.

"I wish they'd jump more out of the water," my mother complained. "You have to look so fast. and they blend right in."

My mother is going to bring a list of complaints with her to give to Saint Peter when she assaults the pearly gates of heaven. I swear she is.

Kai's voice on the loudspeaker overran my mother's. "Ocean conservation starts with connection. We believe that, as we build personal relationships with the ocean and its wildlife, we become more invested stewards of the marine environment. Whales, as individuals, have compelling stories to tell: where will this humpback migrate this winter to give birth? Did the whale with scars from a propeller incident survive another year? What happened to the entangled whale I saw in the news?"

"Look!" yelled a passenger. "I just saw a blow over there! Look! I know I did! I'm sure of it!"

Kai continued, "For science, unique identifiable markings on a whale's flukes—that's the tail, folks—and on the dorsal fin allow us to non-invasively track whale movements and stories over time. By focusing on whales, we bring attention to the marine ecosystem as a whole and the challenges we face as a global community."

"He sounds like a nice young man," my mother remarked. "He sounds American."

Don't take the bait, I told myself. *Don't take the bait.*

I took the bait.

"Ali is American," I said. "He was born in Boston."

9

"But his parents weren't," she said, with something like relish. "I just wish you could find a nice—"

I cut her off. "Ali is a nice American man," I said.

"But why would his parents even come to America?" my mother asked, for possibly the four-thousandth time. "Everyone should just stay home. Where they belong."

Breathe, Riley. Just breathe. "I think they would have liked to stay home," I said, trying to keep my voice steady. "There was just the minor inconvenience of a civil war. Makes it difficult to enjoy your morning coffee when there's a bomb explosion next door. Seriously, Ma, don't you *hate* it when that happens?"

"You're taking a tone with me," my mother said. "Don't take a tone with me."

Kai saved me yet again. "That's a good question," his voice said over the loudspeaker. "For those of you who didn't hear, this gentleman just asked how we know these whales by name. Of course, these are just names *we* give to them—they have their own communication systems and ways of identifying themselves and each other! So as I said, these are whales that return to the marine sanctuary every summer. Many of them are females, who can be counted on to bring their new calves up to Stellwagen Bank because they can feast on nutritious sand lance—that's a tiny fish humpbacks just love—and teach their offspring to hunt. Together with Allied Whale in Bar Harbor at the College of the Atlantic, the Center for Coastal Studies Humpback Whale Research Group runs a study of return rates of whales based on decades of sighting data. So, in other words, we get to see the same whales, year after year. The first one ever named was a female we called Salt." He didn't say what I knew: that Allied Whale and the Center for Coastal Studies didn't always play well together. For one thing, they had totally different names for the same whales. I managed to keep that fact to myself.

"Your father will wish he came along," my mother said.

My father, to the best of my knowledge, was sitting out by the pool at the Race Point Inn, reading a newspaper and drinking a Bloody Mary. My mother was the dogged tourist in the family: when we'd gone on family vacations together, she was the one who found all the museums and statues and sights-of-interest to visit. She practically memorized guidebooks. My father, bemused, went along with most of it, though his idea of vacation was more centered around doing as little as possible for as much time as possible.

Retirement didn't seem to have changed that in any significant way.

"You're here until Sunday," I pointed out. "You can take him out."

She sniffed. "He doesn't know anything about whales," she said.

"Then that's the point. He'll learn." Okay, come on, give me a little credit: I was *really trying* here.

"Maybe," she said darkly. "What are those other boats out there?"

I looked. "Some of them are just private boats. And a lot of the fishing charters come out here," I said. "And when there are whales spotted, they come and look, too. Gives the customers an extra thrill." I knew from Kai and a couple of the other naturalists that the whale-watch people weren't thrilled with the extra attention: the private boats in particular didn't always maintain safe distances from the whales. Once a whale was spotted and one or two of the Dolphin Fleet stopped to look, anyone within sight followed their lead. It could get quite crowded on a summer day.

And dangerous. There had been collisions in the past—boats on boats and, once that I knew of, a boat hitting a whale. Some days it was enough to despair of the human race.

Kai was talking. "Well, folks, this is a real treat! The whale that just blew on our port side is Piano, who's a Stellwagen regular easy to identify for some unfortunate reasons, because she has both vessel propeller strike *and* entanglement scars. This whale is a survivor, however, and has been a regular on Stellwagen for years!" Amazing, I thought cynically, she even gave us the time of day after all that.

"I didn't see the scars," said my mother.

We waited around for a little while and then felt the engines start up again and the deck vibrate. I didn't like the feeling. I knew exactly how irrational my fear was, and knowing did nothing to alleviate it. I'd had some bad experiences out on the water in the past, and that vibration brought them all back. I'd tried getting over it by occasionally renting a small sailboat with my friend Thea, but—well, again, I always thought I'd be able to swim to shore from the sailboat if anything went wrong. Not out here.

And then there was the whole not-letting-my-mother-know side to things. If she did, she'd never let me hear the end of it.

At least when we were talking about whales we weren't talking about her ongoing matrimonial hopes for me, the matrimonial successes of (it seemed) all her friends' offspring, and the bitter disappointment she was feeling around my approaching middle age without a husband in tow. That seemed to be where all our conversations began... and ended.

And I *wasn't* approaching middle age. Forty is the new thirty, and all that sort of thing.

"The captain says we have another pair coming up, folks, off to the port side now... I'm just checking them out... it's a whale called Milkweed and her new calf! Mom is traveling below the surface right now, but you can see the calf rolling around here..." There was a pause and a murmur and then his voice came back. "No, that's not abnormal. The baby's learning everything it needs to know about buoyancy and swimming, and you can be sure Mom's always close by. We're going to slowly head back toward Cape Cod now..." And, a moment later, "Looks like Milkweed and the baby are staying with us! Folks, as you're seeing here, whales can be just as curious about us as we are about them! What Milkweed is doing now—see her, on the starboard side, at three o'clock—we call it spy-hopping."

"Why on earth would they be curious about us?" wondered my mother.

"That," I said, looking at her and knowing she'd never get the sarcasm, "is a really good question."

Just breathe, Riley. Just breathe.

2

It was hot in town.

You forget the heat when you've been out on the water. They tell you to bring a sweater—my mother and I had naturally argued about it before embarking on the trip—and it really is quite pleasant once you pass the breakwater and round Long Point. But Provincetown itself was in full summer swing, which means hordes of people treating Commercial Street as a pedestrian mall (it isn't, but tell that to the people who scowl when you try to drive down it), and the smell of frying food, slightly sickening, in the air.

Sydney's First Rule of Tourism: They absolutely lose their peripheral vision when they travel. I know this, because as I observe

Commercial Street, what I'm seeing is no one notices anyone else in their immediate vicinity. Step to the right or to the left, don't look, it doesn't matter someone's coming by on a bicycle or someone else has stopped in front of you. Just do whatever you want.

Provincetown is where Immediate Gratification comes when it goes on vacation.

I managed to dodge one family group and one couple all hell-bent on hitting me ("ramming speed, Mr. Sulu," as Captain Kirk might have said) and make it more or less unscathed to the post office to check my mail. I looked nostalgically at the Canteen—my idea for a nice solo dinner tonight, but not while my parents were in town—and headed back to the inn.

The inn's owner, Glenn, was sitting in the lobby lounge area with a glass of Scotch. And my father. They were both laughing when I walked in, looking cool as the proverbial cucumbers while I was all hot and bothered from the sun and the crowd and the humid eighty-five degrees it was outside, and for a moment it was as though an Edwardian snapshot had drifted down through time to land in my hand. *Portrait of Gentlemen Enjoying an Afternoon Beverage* followed by *Portrait of Gentlemen's Afternoon Disturbed by Woman Employee.*

"Ah, Sydney!" Glenn looked at me indulgently. My father is not a small man, but Glenn managed to dwarf him all the same. Glenn is a member of a tribe we call "bears": mostly large, hairy gay men who love other large, hairy gay men, all of them projecting an appealing image of rugged masculinity. Don't knock it. There are a lot of relationships based on far fewer points of commonality.

"Hey, Glenn. Hey, Dad." I flopped down in the other armchair, grateful for the air conditioning. "It's hot out."

"Where's your mother?" my father wanted to know.

"Huh? I thought she'd be back here. I just went to pick up my mail at the post office."

"Did you have a nice time?"

I nodded. "Sure. There were dolphins coming into the harbor, they ran with us for a while." My father looked polite and Glenn grinned. He loves the dolphins.

"It's the best whale-watching outfit anywhere," Glenn told my father. "They single-handedly brought whale-watching to the East Coast. Everyone else is an imitation."

"I'm sure he's impressed," I said to Glenn and stood up. "I'm going to get a drink, either of you need another round?"

"Why not?" my father asked, sounding mildly surprised at his own daring.

I headed into the first of the several bars the Race Point keeps open—and filled—all summer. This was a smallish one just off the lobby, before you get to the restaurant or the dining rooms or the patio, and only two people were sitting there. I snagged my father's Scotch ("no water, no soda, no ice, no contamination of a good drink") and got myself a Mojito, which seemed to fit with the heat of the day better than my usual glass of Côtes du Rhône. "Thanks, Bill."

"We live to serve," the bartender quipped, and I headed back to the lobby. My mother had joined the merry band by now, and looked a little askance at the glasses in my hands. "I'll get you something," I promised her, put them down, and headed to the bar again.

When I got back to the lobby, my mother was sipping my drink. "What do you call this? It's good."

"Mojito. I'll trade you." I handed her gin and tonic over, rescued my cocktail, and sat down. "You look like you had a good day out on the water," my father said.

My mother put a hand to her hair. "I must look a fright," she said automatically, waiting.

It's a call-and-response routine they have down pat. "Not at all," said my father. "You always look sensational." Having fulfilled his obligation, he buried his nose in his glass without any further ado.

"Thank you so much," my mother purred.

I looked at Glenn and rolled my eyes. How long had my parents been here? Only a couple of days? It felt like it had passed the two-year mark by now. He cleared his throat and tried to keep from laughing; all he managed was a somewhat unpleasant smirk. "What are your plans for the evening?"

"We have reservations at the Mews," I put in. The upside to my parents visiting is they like to eat out. A lot. For me, that meant a lot of nice dinners I couldn't normally afford.

The downside to my parents visiting? Everything else.

At least I'd be able to order my favorite, the Vietnamese Shaking Beef. I could almost taste it already.

My mother sipped her drink and regarded me over the rim of the glass. "Is Mirela joining us?" For someone whose whole emotional life seemed to center on my matrimonial plans—or lack thereof—she let my friend Mirela off the hook completely. It was annoying. Mirela even has a child, which you'd think would raise the marriage stakes higher in my mother's mind. But, no. Mirela's an *artiste*.

"Not tonight," I said. "Tomorrow night. She's off to the theater tonight."

"What's playing?" asked Glenn. He always asks, never goes. It's more to sound like he is *au fait* with the theatre community (which, granted, is sizeable) than to pretend any real interest in the plays themselves. In the summer, you can see excellent live theater at (at least) two places in Provincetown, one in Truro, two in Wellfleet, one in Brewster and two or three in Dennis. Not bad for what is essentially a rural area.

I didn't have to consult any program: I keep up with theatre as a matter of course. Tourists ask. "Chekov," I said. "Mirela loves Chekov."

"Who doesn't?" asked Glenn flippantly, and my father looked at him, briefly appraising.

My mother said, "I never understood what all those Russians were talking about. Probably about snow. Give me a nice English or American play anytime. Something in a language you can understand!"

"You know you're supposed to see Russian plays in *translation*, right?" I asked. With my mother, you have to.

"Don't you take a tone with me, Sydney Riley."

Yep: everything was back to normal.

***

In the end, I never got to eat my Vietnamese Shaking Beef. Or anything else on the Mews' menu.

My mother was halfway through explaining to my father—who didn't care—and Glenn—who already knew—how humpback whales don't have teeth at all despite being so big, when one of Glenn's Handsome Young Things (he and Mike the manager seem to have an endless supply of gorgeous young men to work all over the inn during the season) came in and tapped Glenn on the shoulder. He said something, rapidly, into Glenn's ear, and that, folks, brought us to the end of our Carefree Segment of the evening.

He looked around immediately and of course so did I, and it was Julie Agassi who was standing by Reception, waiting. Julie.

Who investigates crime. I won't say my antennae went up; I'll just say I was mildly interested as Glenn excused himself and headed over to meet Julie.

"Must be an important guest," hazarded my mother, looking after him. "Look at her, Sydney: would you say that's a lesbian?" Even after all these years I've lived in P'town, my mother still infuriatingly behaves like we're all in a zoo and she's the visitor.

"She is important," I agreed. "And she is a lesbian."

"You can tell by looking at her?" I'd come close to amazing my mother.

"Well… no. I know her. She's the head of detectives at the Provincetown Police," I said.

My mother scowled at me and drank some of her gin and tonic. My father fingered the copy of the *Cape Cod Times* sitting next to him but didn't quite dare open it. Julie was telling Glenn something he didn't want to hear. She glanced over at me once or twice, nodded, and left after a longish pause. I wondered if she was waiting for me to join them. That would be something new and unexpected—Julie usually doesn't involve me in crimes.

Not intentionally, anyway.

Glenn stood by reception for another few moments, staring at nothing in particular, before coming back to us. "So sorry, Mrs. Riley, Mr. Riley, but I have some things to attend to." He reached for his glass and drained the remaining finger of Scotch.

"Is everything all right?" my mother asked. I hate it when people say that in fiction or the movies—if there's occasion to ask the question, then the answer's a foregone conclusion, at least as far as I'm concerned—and I hated it even more coming from my mother. "Ma, it's clearly not. Why don't we let Glenn deal with it? Don't you want to freshen up before dinner?"

"I will say, being out at sea does a lot for your appetite," she said. "I'm famished."

"Go get ready," I urged, capitalizing on what might be movement. "You've got about an hour before we have to leave."

"Maybe I'll lie down for a few minutes," said my mother. "Edward? What do you think?"

"About what, dear?" My father had dispatched his Scotch with some alacrity when no one was looking.

"Should I lie down before supper?"

My father gave me the sort of amazed look he's been giving me my whole life. What amazes *me* is that after all this time *he* continues to be amazed. "If that's what you'd like to do," he said cautiously, looking for a trap.

"I think I'll lie down," she decided with finality. "Sydney, I hope you're going to change your clothes."

"No one dresses for dinner in P'town, Ma," I protested.

"*We* do. Now go. Come pick us up when it's time to leave."

"Okay," I said. I couldn't imagine what she thought I was going to pick her up in. My Honda, known far and wide as The Little Green Car, scarcely left the expensive parking-spot I'd snagged for it up at the Monument on

High Pole Hill. And the Mews was only about two blocks away from the inn, with absolutely no parking…

The important thing was they were heading toward the stairs at the back of the room, and I grabbed my mojito—I do have priorities—and headed into Glenn's office. "What's going on?"

He'd been doing absolutely nothing when I went in, slumped in the chair behind his big desk, staring at the landline that was, as far as I could tell, not doing anything untoward. "Glenn?"

He roused himself and looked at me. Or through me. "That was Julie," he said.

"Yes. I saw her. What's going on, Glenn?"

"It's Vincent," he said. He shook his head, fast, as if dismissing thoughts he didn't want to entertain. "Vincent Almada."

"Okay." The name was vaguely familiar, in the way a lot of Portuguese surnames are familiar in P'town. We used to be a fishing port, first stop for families leaving the Azores, coming to places like New Bedford and Gloucester

26

and Provincetown, first to fish and then to establish a life.

"He owns the fleet."

"What fleet?" No one owned P'town's decimated commercial fishing industry, just a few hardened souls determined to keep going, people with names like Silva and Costa and Medeiros. And Almada, come to that. "Oh!" I'd just gotten it. "You mean the *Dolphin* Fleet!" The very whale watch I'd just been on an hour before. "What about him?"

He looked at me but I didn't have the sense he was looking at anything in particular. As if he were distracted, trying to remember a line from a poem, doing sums in his head. "He's been kidnapped."

"Kidnapped?" It was probable that echoing everything Glenn said wasn't particularly helpful. It was also true I didn't know what else to say.

Glenn nodded. "Julie just told me."

"Why?" He could take that any way he liked. Why did she tell you? Why was Vincent kidnapped? Either one would be a good start.

"Has there been a demand?" I was feeling a little nauseated. He probably wouldn't notice.

He nodded again. "I don't know where they thought the money's coming from," he said heavily. "There are people in town who could raise that much. Not the Almadas."

I tried to follow his thread. "Because people look at the Dolphin Fleet and assume the family's rich?"

"That's probably it," Glenn said.

I finally remembered I had a drink in my hand and took a swallow, fast. "Are you friends with them?" I asked. "The Almada family?"

He looked at me. "He saved my life."

Wait, what? I thought Mike and I were the only ones around in the lifesaving business. Well, besides the EMTs and the clinic staff and… "What happened?"

"It was a couple of years before you came to town," said Glenn. He sounded, suddenly, exhausted. "I got sick. Needed a new kidney. I wasn't living here then, just hanging out summers. No one could help. No one in

Chicago, no one from my family, not even Barry, and believe me, he tried, he had them test him twice. No possible donors."

I imagined Barry, my former boss and Glenn's longtime companion, and how hysterical he'd have been. Barry had adored Glenn. The only thing good about his murder was he hadn't had to outlive his partner: the loss, the grief, would have consumed him. Barry would have moved heaven and earth to get Glenn that transplant. "And Vincent was a match?"

He nodded. "Vincent was a match," he said. "Everything went fine. They did it right at Cape Cod Hospital. His family—there was some feeling at the time. About me not being family, about me not being Portuguese. About me being gay." He looked troubled. "Vincent—he ignored it all. Boasted about it down the Old Colony Tap, the way I understood it. Said he'd saved a life. Said it wiped his slate clean."

"What slate?" I asked curiously.

Glenn shrugged. "Who knows?" he asked rhetorically. "Barry and me, we were just glad there was someone, and that the surgery went well and we could all put it behind us. I always send him a thank-you card every year on the anniversary. I always remember."

"Does everyone else?"

"Hmm? What do you mean?"

"Well," I said, "there's some reason Julie Agassi came all the way out here to tell you about it. She's not exactly free and generous with her information at the best of times." And didn't I know it: as the town's unofficial sleuth, I was always asking Julie questions.

Once in a great while she even answered them.

I was running my fingers over my mental file folders, trying to think of what I knew about the family that owns the Dolphin Fleet. Mostly I knew old stories, how the Avellar family had started the activity and had gone from one single recreational fishing charter boat to owning a fleet that spent summers in P'town and winters holed up in Fairhaven across the inlet from New Bedford. How the whale watches had started as a way for a charter boat captain to extend the season and attract a different crowd of tourists. How they'd invited Stormy Mayo from the Center for Coastal Studies to be the first naturalist. Stormy was a plankton guy in those days; he learned about whales and dolphins and sea birds as he went along.

The Avellars had sold the Dolphin Fleet to third or fourth or something cousins, the Almadas. And I knew practically nothing about *them*.

Besides, there was another unwelcome thought creeping up behind that one. I clung to Vincent, making my brain think about who would know him and who would decide the family could afford a ransom. That's all this was about. A man. *This is about Vincent. This is only about Vincent. Breathe, Riley. Just breathe.*

Glenn was watching me. "Julie told me because she knows my connection to Vincent," he said.

"Or because you can raise the money?" It was a crass thing to say and I knew it.

"Possibly," he acknowledged. He was frowning. "Sydney, what's going on? You look like you've seen a ghost."

A lithe one, young and pretty, just darting behind the desk, leaving nothing but a smothered giggle in the air. I swallowed. "We can't tell my parents," I managed to say.

"I wasn't going to," he said, "Sydney, what *is* it?"

I ran my tongue over my lips. "Because," I said, "my sister was kidnapped. And we never saw her again."

3

I don't know which of us was more startled by my outburst. Glenn, because it was so sudden and unexpected... or me, for pretty much the same reasons. I just opened my mouth and the words came out.

The slim pretty ghost giggled again in the still room. I couldn't believe she was still hanging around after all this time.

"You'd better sit down," said Glenn. He opened his bottom desk drawer and brought out the Laphroaig and two glasses. I shivered when I accepted the drink, but the whiskey spread inside then, warm and calming, and I felt better. "I'm sorry," I said. "I didn't mean for that to come out."

"What happened?" he asked, his voice and eyes steady.

I swirled the liquid, looking at it and not at him. "Alexandra," I said. "Alex."

Saying her name out loud after years of feeling good, getting through days and even weeks without thinking about her. Alexandra, ten years older than me, always with an unattainable nonchalant sophistication she wore as casually as her eclectic thrift-store clothing. My mother, on her case about it: "People will think we can't afford to get you the right clothes."

Alex, amused. "These are my right clothes," she said. "The textile industry is the second-highest contributor to global warming."

"Don't you change the subject, Alexandra Riley!"

I found her out in the gargantuan space they called a garage in this neighborhood, crying, sitting on an old toolbox. I don't know whose it was; my parents' immediate response to all things mechanical is to "call the guy."

That there is always a guy is unquestioned in their world.

"What's wrong, Alex?" I was eight years old; older sisters aren't supposed to get upset. "Don't cry!"

She pulled me close to her, blotting her smudged mascara and eyeliner all over my sleeve. Funny, the things you remember. I held onto that shirt for years, and I never washed it, either. "Ma's ready to kill me."

"She'll get over it," I said automatically. She always did, no matter what it was. There was a pattern: we had to suffer through a bout of icy anger, and then she moved on and we could, too.

Alex was shaking her head. "Not this," she whispered.

I looked at her curiously. "What did you do wrong?"

"It wasn't wrong," she said immediately, in a voice that assured me it was very wrong indeed. She sniffled a little more. "Sydney, I might be going away for a while."

"Can I come, too?"

She smiled; I remember that smile. Smiling through the tears. "Not this time," she said.

"Why not?" I must have been at the age when everything needed to be explored. No question too detailed; no detail overlooked.

"Because it's about the next thing," she said, mysteriously. "The next thing for me, not *your* next thing."

"What's my next thing?"

Another smile, another sniffle. "I don't know, pumpkin."

"So what's yours?"

"Go inside," she said.

"I don't want to."

"Just *go inside*, Sydney."

I did. And I never saw her again.

The story came together slowly, over time. First it was Alex had gone to Boston to work for a modeling agency; I was quite ready to believe that—she was the most beautiful person I knew. And it was actually true, as far as it went… she'd met someone at a party. He told her she had great cheekbones. Yeah, all the usual predictable predatory nonsense, but she was naïve and it worked. She wanted to get out of New Hampshire.

She was eager to stretch, to get things started, to move onward and forward into the excitement of her real life. She wanted to reach for whatever horizon lay before her. One chapter finished, with a line firmly drawn under it; the next chapter tantalizingly just out of reach. Alexandra wanted to catch hold of it, like a ring on a merry-go-round, grab the future with both hands.

Our parents, naturally, said absolutely not. But she was eighteen. She left that night.

Now I looked at Glenn. "They wanted money, of course," I said, my voice surprisingly steady. "I mean, it's possible she was originally going to get trafficked. At least, that's what Ali thought when I told him about it; but maybe he said it just because it's what he does." Ali worked for ICE, in the human-trafficking department. "She really *was* beautiful. So he could be right. But all we knew was they contacted us, they said they were holding her—I remember that word, because to my mind it sounded gentle, holding her, maybe that wasn't so bad, you know?—and they wanted money to give her back." I shrugged. "Maybe they were never going to give her back. Maybe that part was too dangerous for them, maybe it would have meant getting caught. I don't know. All I know is, they were holding her in some kind of crappy housing somewhere in Allston." Allston was a Boston neighborhood, known for cheap rents for Boston University students, five to an apartment, transient as hell. "They did the thing you see on TV—you know, took pictures of her holding that day's newspaper to show the date."

I had never been allowed to see those pictures.

I cleared my throat. "Anyway, my father— well, he's rich compared to most people, but he's not super-rich, you know, he doesn't own islands or yachts or racehorses or anything like that—but he was getting the money. He was going to pay them.

He was going to pay them. That was the phrase I remembered from those days, the FBI camped out with machines and electrical cords in the great room, my father tense on the telephone with banks, with friends, with colleagues. He was going to pay them.

"No one knew what went wrong," I told Glenn. "It didn't make sense. Everything was arranged. Maybe they panicked. Maybe she tried to get away and things got out of hand." That was another odd expression—things got out of hand. Poor silly sweet Alexandra. Things just got out of hand.

Serious people at the door, going into my father's study with my parents, my mother's voice rising in a wail that sounded for all the world like an animal in pain. Sitting on the stairs with the young FBI agent who'd been assigned to look after me, her voice steady. "I need you to be very brave, Sydney... here you go. Breathe, can you do that for me? Just take one deep breath? That's good. See, that helps. Take another one, deep in your belly... Breathe, just breathe..."

Breathe, Riley. "It was thirty years ago," I said to Glenn. "We don't talk about her much." Or, in fact, at all.

He was looking pale. "I don't know what to say."

I shrugged. "Who does?" I asked, aiming for flippancy.

He was staring at me longer than was comfortable. "I'm not saying this is going to end up the same way," I said, quickly, possibly misinterpreting his expression. "I'm just saying, my parents…"

"Yeah, of course," he said. There was a long fraught silence, and I couldn't listen to it, hear the haunting silvery laughter still shimmering in the air between us. "I don't really remember her that much," I confessed quickly to fill the air, fill the space. "We were so far apart in years, we didn't go to the same schools or have any of the same friends." I couldn't even remember Alex's friends, though I did remember they came to our house a lot, and there was loud music and my mother always yelling at her to leave her bedroom door open when she had visitors…

I jerked myself back into the present. "What did they say?" I asked. "About Vincent?"

He swallowed. "They sent a picture from a pay-as-you-go burner phone," he said. "Of him holding today's newspaper."

That was it. The room tilted around me, like the deck of the whale boat, and there was a loud ringing in my ears. I grabbed the Scotch and poured some down my throat.

Glenn was still talking. "They told Julie to bring it here. Because they know."

"Know what?"

He looked at me steadily and then said my father's words. "That I'm going to pay them."

And then I really did pass out.

***

"You're not pregnant, are you?" It was my mother's voice.

I struggled back slowly into consciousness. "What?"

"Are you pregnant?"

Several dark blobs coalesced and resolved themselves into her face. I was lying on the sofa in Glenn's office, and my mother was perched on the edge of it beside me. "Well, *are* you?"

"No, Ma."

"That's when healthy young women faint, you know. Maybe you should take a test. One of those ones you do at home. I don't know why else you would faint."

Glenn said, "Mrs. Riley? Here's some water."

My mother took the glass from his hand and took a sip. "Thank you," she said.

I managed to catch Glenn's eye. *You see what I deal with?* I think he was about to tell her the water had been meant for me, but decided it wasn't worth the struggle. Glenn's a smart man.

"How is she?" My father's voice.

"I think she's pregnant," my mother told him.

"Oh, for heaven's sake," I said in exasperation and struggled to a sitting position. "I'm not pregnant, I'm fine, I've just had a long day."

"So did I, but you don't see me fainting."

I looked at her. "You're made of stronger stuff than I am, Ma."

"Are you sure you're all right?" My father again, willing everything to be fine so he could go back to his vacation.

"I'm sure," I said. "You two go to dinner. I'll just rest for a bit."

"We couldn't possibly go without you, Sydney." My mother as martyr. "How could we possibly enjoy the meal?"

Nothing short of the four horsemen of the Apocalypse would keep *me* from enjoying the Mews' Vietnamese Shaking Beef if I were sitting in front of it. "Go, Ma. Really. I'll see you tomorrow."

"If you're sure…" My father couldn't have sounded more relieved if he'd tried.

"Go," I said, making flapping motions with my hand. "I'm fine, seriously. I'll see you in the morning."

My mother allowed herself one more rear-action battery. "I still say you should take the test," she said darkly.

"*Go*, Ma." Go before I do something violent. *Breathe, Riley, breathe...*

The room was abnormally quiet when they left.

I sighed and drank some of the water she'd left behind. "Sorry, Glenn. I didn't see that coming."

"Of course not. Are you really okay?"

I nodded. "It's funny, isn't it—I haven't thought of her in months." The last time I'd talked about Alex, I'd been curled up in front of the fireplace in Ali's apartment in Boston three or four years ago, his arm around me, and I'd told the story to the flames, not looking at him. Maybe I still was wound a little tightly about it, but I hadn't fainted. I didn't even know this Vincent guy...

"I'll have Peter drive you home," Glenn was saying, picking up the phone on his desk.

"No," I said. "I'll walk. Clear my head." He started to say something, and I held up my hand. "Don't you start in on me, too," I warned. "I'm walking home now, and tomorrow I'm coming back and I'm going to help you and Julie."

He raised his eyebrows, slowing replacing his phone on the desk. "And you're going to do this how, exactly, without your parents finding out?"

"I'm still working on that," I told him.

42

I got up and the room wasn't tilting any-more, which was a definite improvement. "Spent too much time at sea today is all," I said.

"Yeah, that must be it."

I stopped at the door and turned back. "It's going to be okay, Glenn," I said. "They'll let him go. Everyone's better at this now than they were thirty years ago." I didn't know that for sure, but it stood to reason.

"I know," he said.

"He's no use to them dead."

"I know."

Impulsively, I walked over and put my arms around him in the closest I could get to a bear hug when you're hugging a bear. "It will be all right," I said softly in the general prox-imity of his ear.

"I know."

But neither of us did, not really, and all the way home I stared at the tourists and the rev-elers, Commercial Street thrumming with the excitement of the start of a summer night, when anything could happen, the magic and the anticipation almost tangible in the air, and I wondered what my poor lost sister would have made of it all.

I waited until I was in the space that passes for an apartment I call home before calling Ali. I needed the comfort, sure; but Ali's in law enforcement, he works in people trafficking for Immigration and Customs Enforcement, and while that probably wasn't what had happened here—I couldn't imagine any competent trafficker thinking there might be a market for sixty-year-old Portuguese men—Ali would still have some professional wisdom to share.

"*Cara.* I was just thinking of you." Ali thinks he's sexy when he speaks Italian. He's right.

I could picture him, the dark fringe of hair falling over his forehead, the ever-present designer stubble on his chin, the gorgeous olive skin, the impossibly deep eyes. "Of course you were," I said automatically. "What are you wearing?"

I obviously hadn't put my usual lightheartedness into the teasing words. "What's wrong?" he asked, fast, his voice sharp.

"Just a little professional consultation," I said. I gave up trying to balance the iPhone on my shoulder, hit the speaker button, and set it on the counter while I opened a bottle of wine. Screw-top. I needed immediate gratification, and tonight seemed like a Merlot night anyway.

"What's up?"

I told him about Glenn and Barry and the kidney Vincent had donated that saved

Glenn's life. I told him about the whale watch boats and the expression on Julie's face when she told Glenn about the kidnapping. I told him Glenn had said, it didn't matter what they asked, he'd find the money. Provincetown is chock-a-block with money if you just know where to look.

"And it reminded you of Alexandra," said Ali. We hadn't talked about her since the first time I'd told him the story.

"Yeah, well," I said, trying to minimize it. I took a fast swallow of wine. "My mother thinks I'm pregnant."

"What!" That startled him, all right.

"Never mind," I said soothingly. "She just can't imagine why else anyone would faint." Fainting is not, but *not*, in my mother's repertoire.

"Oh, right. You were doing the whale watch with her today." He was still playing catch-up. "Does she know?"

"About Vincent? No. I can't let them know, either." I'd been eight when Alexandra was kidnapped and killed; I was almost peripheral to the event. Our parents had been... well, *parents*. The people who were supposed to keep her safe. Not for the first time, I marveled their marriage had held together. The guilt must have been nearly unbearable.

"No, I can see that," he acknowledged. "Maybe this is one you need to sit out, *cara*."

He knew me too well. "It's *Glenn*," I said.

"And Julie's on the case," Ali added. "She knows what she's doing. And it won't be hers exclusively, anyway. Most police chiefs formally invite the feds in on kidnapping cases, and I'd be surprised if Provincetown didn't."

"Oh, God. You're right." The FBI at the inn. What a great way to keep my parents in the dark.

"Take your folks up-Cape," Ali suggested. "Walk around Heritage Gardens in Sandwich. Do the canal tour."

"And not help Glenn? I don't think so," I countered.

"*Cara*, forgive me, but you forget what you do for a living. You're a wedding planner. You're not in law enforcement."

"I'm his *friend*."

He sighed. Ali knows which battles are worth fighting. "Can you send them home?"

"Are you forgetting? This is my *mother* we're talking about. Oh, and I'm not, by the way."

"Not what?"

"Pregnant."

"Well," he said, not missing a beat, "I'm relieved to hear it. One small child in the family is enough."

There it was. The family. The family we're not born into; the family we choose. There are a lot of families like that in Provincetown. Ali was my family, and so was Glenn, and so was Mirela and her adopted daughter Lily. And Mike, the inn's manager, currently taking a sabbatical studying something-or-other in Switzerland. And… "That's just it," I said. "I can't see Glenn go through this alone. I have to help."

"Well," he said philosophically, "maybe Mirela can entertain your parents."

"Not without my mother trying to marry her off," I said, and the mood lifted, and we both laughed.

It was a complicated scenario any way you looked at it. And it was about to become a lot more complicated.

Because the next day saw the return of Guy Husband.

4

He turned up at the inn.

I was sitting at the desk in the glorified closet they call my office back behind Reception, returning emails and swearing under my breath. I do a lot of that. All wedding planners do, as they grapple with what happens when a couple's fantasies come up against reality ("no, you may not release twenty doves into the air during the ceremony") and the disappointment all becomes, somehow, my fault.

The current Handsome Young Man at reception called back to me. "Sydney? Someone here to see you."

I pressed send on my latest missive and stood up. And nearly fainted for the second day in a row. "Guy," I said, my voice wary.

He smiled. "Hello, Sydney. It's been a frightfully long time, how are you?"

It had been close to a year and a half, to be more precise. He was still handsome, elegant, and very English. "I'm fine," I said. I didn't ask how he'd been. I didn't really care.

Holly Folly is Provincetown's winter holiday celebration, when we trim trees, watch a Santa Speedo Run (you couldn't make this stuff up), cheer as a "lobster pot tree" made of lobster traps and decorated with bows and lights goes up, and generally make merry. At one very remarkable Holly Folly, Guy Husband (yeah, that's his real name), Mr. We'll-Find-Shipwrecks-While-You-Wait, had been in town. He found the wreck he'd been looking for in the frigid Atlantic off the tip of the Cape, and found what he hadn't been looking for, a relationship with my friend Mirela.

Well, we'd all thought it was a relationship. Guy apparently had had other ideas. He'd disappeared once the wreck was secured, and though people from his outfit had been back to the Cape and were still diving it, the man himself had never returned.

Mirela had had some really bad times after that—you don't leave a young Bulgarian at the equivalent of the altar without some fallout—and so it was perfectly understandable under the circumstances I was less than delighted to have Guy back in P'town.

He got it. Something flitted across his face, an expression of pain perhaps, something errant and shadowy, and then he cleared his throat. "Before you tell me I'm persona non grata, which you have every right to do, tell me how Mirela is."

"How do you *think* she is? No," I said quickly, "never mind. You obviously haven't thought of her at all."

He cleared his throat. "I know it appears that way—"

"Wait—what? There's another way to see it? You left without a word, you broke her heart, and now it just *seems* you weren't thinking of her? That's a good one." I took a breath. "She's fine, she's happy, and you'd better not be here to change that."

"It isn't my intention," he said. "Sydney. Can I have a word? In private? I owe—well, and the very least, I owe you all an apology."

"Not to me," I snapped. "I don't care about you one way or the other. But, sure, you can tell me about how much you missed her and I can tell you about how you're not coming within a mile of seeing her." I came out from behind Reception and gestured for him to follow me.

He looked good, I had to admit. He was still a triple-threat in the looks department: tall, dark, and handsome, wearing pale linen trousers and a startling purple button-down shirt, a flowered tie that picked up both colors to a T. I'd forgotten that about him: no matter where you were or what you were doing, Guy always looked like he fit the occasion perfectly and everyone else was either over- or under-dressed. It was late June, and hot, so I'd been casual about my appearance: a sleeveless summer dress, flats, my hair in a ponytail. No makeup. Standing next to Guy, there was a voice inside my head saying, I told you so, a little mascara, that wouldn't have gone amiss.

Actually, the voice sounded a lot like my mother's. Scratch that.

We wandered into the private lounge, a smallish room with a door that could be closed—hence the "private" part. I didn't close it. "So why are you here?" I demanded.

Guy sat down on the loveseat, adjusting his pants at the knee, crossing one leg elegantly over the other. "I was," he said pleasantly, "in prison."

Whoa. Hadn't seen that one coming. Not exactly on my bingo card. I perched cautiously on the edge of a chair. "Okay," I said slowly, drawing the second vowel out. "Do you want to tell me about it?"

"I can't think I have a choice," he said. "It's a long story, of course."

"Aren't they all?"

"But there's no need to go into details. It had to do with my business." Which was probably still locating shipwrecks and bringing up their artifacts. Nice work if you can get it. "The truth is, Sydney, it was a case of extremely poor judgment on my part. I formed a limited partnership with someone who, as it turns out, wasn't to be trusted."

"A lot of that going around," I said tartly.

He didn't react. "We were actually already under investigation when I arrived in Provincetown last year to locate the *Mignonette*," he said, referring to the pirate wreck off Race Point. "And of course that took all my focus. As well as Mirela, of course. I'd meant to go and settle things in New York and then return to see her, to—well, to see if we wanted to continue what we'd begun. But they were waiting for me when I got off the plane." His private plane, I remembered. It had caused quite a stir in town at the time.

"I thought," I said carefully, "everyone gets a phone call when they're arrested."

He raised his eyebrows. "And so I should have rung her?"

"Some contact might have been helpful," I said, shrugging. I took a deep breath. "Come *on*, Guy. See it from our point of view and you'll see why I'm so angry. As far as we knew, you'd just disappeared into thin air. Mirela emailed you, she called, she even wrote some real honest-to-goodness letters on paper before she gave up. Your companies were being run without you—we know, we looked into it." Well, Ali had, at my behest. "You could've been dead, for all we knew. If you cared about her at all, you'd have at least *told* her." After the initial flurry of activity, after talking about him nonstop for about two weeks, after she'd given up, Mirela never mentioned his name again.

"That," he said, "is probably what *you* would have done. And possibly what I *should* have done. But, Sydney, everyone deals with these things in their own way. I was—devastated."

"Because your trust had been misplaced," I said, sarcasm creeping into my voice. "Gosh, I wonder what *that* feels like."

He frowned, but didn't pursue it. "How is Mirela?" he asked instead, and immediately put a hand up to stop me from speaking. "I know what you're thinking. We can take it as read. I know you'd prefer me to disappear and never see her again."

"Something like that," I agreed.

"You have to understand," he said gently, "I need to hear it from her." He paused. "I am perhaps being entirely selfish here, but I cannot just go back to my life and pick up the

pieces without knowing. Knowing whether…
I still have a chance with her. I know there's
fallout everywhere from what I did—personally, professionally, so forth… But I need your
help now, Sydney. I need to tell her."

"Tell her what?"

Guy Husband looked at me. "That I still
love her," he said simply.

***

"He was *where*?" Ali's voice registered in-
credulity.

"In prison," I said again. "A guest of Her
Majesty, as he put it. He got extradited and
spent the past year and a half in West Sussex,
wherever that is. Some prison that used to be
a naval air station, he said."

"Is that relevant? That it used to be a naval
air station?"

"Probably not," I agreed. "Just telling you
what I know."

I was back in my cubbyhole, having sent
Guy Husband away—and he wasn't going far
away, as the Handsome Young Man at reception had helpfully showed me Guy's reservation at the inn—and trying to keep my voice
down.

Ali whistled tunelessly through his teeth,
something he did when thinking something

over. "He didn't go straight to the gallery to see Mirela? Or to her studio?"

"He promised he wouldn't contact her yet. He wanted to—see how to approach her. Asked for my advice." Fat chance *that* would help him; I rarely took it myself. "It's actually kind of endearing. Maybe even the right thing to do, when you think about it." I was reluctant to say so. "For all he knew, she could have gotten married or something in the meantime. This way, if necessary, he could just leave and she'd never know he'd been here."

"You'd have told her."

"There's that," I acknowledged.

"Well, it's something , anyway. Does he know about Lily?"

I shook my head, which is silly when you're on the telephone. "No. I didn't tell him."

"I see." He paused, considering. "How did he seem?"

I thought about it for a moment. I was, begrudgingly enough, coming around to Guy's way of thinking. And he *could* have stayed away; he could have just kept sailing off into the sunset. That said something for his courage, or maybe about how he felt about Mirela... *not* that I was going to let him think I admired him, or anything crazy like that. "He was calm," I said. "Thoughtful."

"Thoughtful? Is that what you said? *Cara*, is that empathy I'm hearing?"

"A momentary lapse," I assured him. "Back to my old cranky self now."

"So what do we do?" Ali asked. That it was "we" was unquestionable; Mirela and he were thick as thieves. Something I was going to take full advantage of.

"You could tell her," I said.

"No. I can't. I'd have to—"

"—come down to the Cape?" I asked. "Gosh, no, you couldn't do that. Not even this weekend." It was Thursday morning.

A sigh. "Yeah, I know," he said at last. "It's the right thing to do."

"Seems like everyone I'm talking to is talking about the right thing to do," I said. "In this case, though, yeah, you're correct. Definitely the right thing to do."

"Hmm. We'll see. All right, I'll head down after work tomorrow. Grab the five-thirty ferry." He paused. "Any more news about— the other thing?"

"Vincent?" I made a face, not that he could see it. "Not really. Glenn's been in his office since before I got here, he's been on the phone, wheeling and dealing."

"But there's been contact with the kidnappers, right? How much are they asking for?"

"Don't know. I didn't want to disturb him, and I have to figure out where to send my parents so they're not around when he's talking about it." Which seemed like all the time.

"Good luck with that. What does Julie say?"

"You know," I said slowly, "If I didn't know better, I'd think you were itching to get involved here."

"Well, since I'm coming down tomorrow…" He laughed, suddenly. "All right. You're right, I'm curious, but only because I want to see if I can help."

"It's not a customs and immigration issue," I said.

"You'd be surprised, *cara*, at what can become a customs and immigration issue. I have to go; I'll see you tomorrow."

"I'll meet the ferry," I promised. "And you know there will be at least one dinner with my parents, don't you?"

"There's a happy thought."

I laughed "Forewarned is forearmed," I said. "Love you."

"*Ti amo, cara.*"

I clicked off and stared at my calendar on the wall. A plan would probably be a good thing. I had my parents to wrangle and entertain, while keeping them in the dark about Vincent. I had Julie and Glenn to consult, because there was no way I wasn't going to be involved in that drama. I had the Guy-and-Mirela thing to think about. Oh, and a couple of weddings looming, to which I really should devote some energy as they represented the only part of the whole thing that actually paid my bills.

My parents would have to come first, as last I'd seen they were in the breakfast room and due to emerge at any moment. I picked up my phone again and scrolled through my contacts until I found the one I was looking for."

"Art's Dune Tours," said a voice on the other end.

"Rob?" I asked. "Hey, it's Sydney Riley from Race Point Inn."

"Sydney! Good to hear from you. How's your season so far?"

"Busy," I said automatically. It's the question we all ask each other from May until October, and the answer is always the same. "Listen, is it too late to arrange something for this morning?"

"Maybe. Maybe not. What do you have in mind?"

"I'm thinking a private tour with a clambake for lunch," I said. "Maybe hook up with the people at the lighthouse for a tour there, too."

"This *morning*?" Art's Dune Tours usually does sunset clambakes.

"Yeah, I know," I said. "Listen, Rob, whatever you need, fine. I know it's last-minute and all. It's just two people." I hesitated. "Um—actually, to tell you the truth, it's for my parents."

He laughed, then. "I see. And you're trying to stash them somewhere while you play detective," he said.

"Play detective?" I asked. "Why, what have you heard's going on?"

"Haven't heard anything," he said cheerfully. "I just know you. All right, I'll do it, but it'll cost you."

"Whatever," I said. "Thanks, Rob."

"Yeah, yeah. Give me an hour to get it together and you can send them over."

"I owe you," I said fervently.

"Oh, you know you do."

One problem solved. Maybe I was on a roll.

5

If I'd been worried about Alexandra hanging around and getting in the way of my detecting, I was wrong. She stayed mercifully out of sight for quite some time.

My mother, who has a sixth sense that's often just a little off, could tell something was going on, though she didn't seem to be able to wrap her head around what it was. I sat down at their table in the breakfast room and announced my plans for their day. "But you're coming too, aren't you?" she asked.

I shook my head. "Have to work, Ma. June's my busiest month." Well, that was true, anyway. "And I've made dinner reservations here at our restaurant," I added quickly, by way of incentive. My father's face lit up. Our restaurant has a Michelin two-star rating, thanks to Adrienne the diva chef who terrifies all and sundry but comes up with the most amazingly wonderful food. My father was constantly asking after her; he seemed to be the only human she didn't terrorize. He'd once gone into the kitchen—taking his life in his hands, as I saw it—to compliment her on her salmon with sorrel (crème fraiche, Sancerre, lemon juice) and had actually emerged alive.

He wasn't about to argue about "dining in." As well he shouldn't. I'd had to bribe Martin the maître d' to give me the reservation.

"What's a dune tour, anyway?" my mother wanted to know. "The dunes? They're taking us out on this trip just so we can look at *sand*?"

"It's a history of the dunes," I said. "You get to learn about nature, Ma."

She snorted. "I have a garden, you know."

"Not quite the same," I said. "Plus, they'll tell you all about the dune shacks—it's these tiny cottages, some of them made out of wood from shipwrecks. Famous people lived out there. Artists and writers." I paused for effect. "Eugene O'Neill," I added enticingly.

"At least that's one playwright's name I can pronounce."

That was a dig at the name I'd bestowed on my cat. "You can pronounce Ibsen," I said, allowing myself to respond when I knew I shouldn't.

My mother had wanted me to name him Pookie.

"Still," she started, and I cut her off. "And the lighthouse," I added a little desperately, not wanting the conversation to stray too far from my plotline. "The lighthouse is beautiful, and it's famous. They made a movie there."

"Who was in it?"

I tried to remember. "Richard Dreyfuss?" I said tentatively.

She shook her head. "He was in *Jaws*," she pronounced.

"Actors generally are in more than one movie, Ma," I said. My father shook his head.

"Don't you take a tone with me, Sydney Riley," she said, right on cue.

"You'll have fun, Ma. Come on. I even got you a pedicab to take you there."

"Your car doesn't work anymore? I told you not to buy a foreign car. Your father's always bought American."

"You're on vacation, Ma. Relax. A pedicab will be fun." The company was owned and run by a group of young Bulgarians, who along with half the student population of the country—or so it felt—come to Provincetown in the summers. They work three, four, five jobs, sleep fifteen to a room, and are a big part of the summer scenery. Mirela was Bulgarian; she too had come for a summer, but stayed on as her career was flourishing here. She was even an American citizen now.

"Come on, Frances," said my father unexpectedly, getting up from the table. "Sydney has work to do. Let's go on this tour."

Once in a great while, he surprised me.

I waved goodbye as they got settled into the pedicab, and as soon as they were spirited down Commercial Street, I knocked on Glenn's door. "It's me," I said, poking my head in. "Oh! Sorry, didn't know…"

There were two people occupying his guest chairs, and immediately I knew— without knowing—who they were.

The feds had arrived.

Glenn waved me in. "Sydney Riley," he said, "This is Special Agent James Nuñez, Special Agent Rosa Dartle." There was no actual reason to think they were FBI; he was wearing slacks and a green polo shirt; she had on shorts, a t-shirt, and flip-flops. But I spend enough time around law-enforcement types— not only is Ali in the field, but his sister Karen is Boston's police commissioner, and Julie Agassi is a friend—to know.

Of course, the gun the Nuñez guy was carrying in the small of his back did rather give things away, too. I could tell it was there by the way he was sitting. Got that from Karen, too.

We all shook hands and I perched on the edge of the sofa. "Sydney knows why you're here," Glenn said to his visitors. He sounded exhausted. "She has some experience."

"With abductions?" asked Agent Nuñez, his voice skeptical.

"Yes," I said, before Glenn could say anything. "I'm just here to help, if I can."

"And what is it you do?"

"I'm the inn's events planner," I said, and, "I want her here," said Glenn at the same time.

They weren't happy about it—oddly enough, most people don't rate event planners very high on the detecting scale—but they needed to work with Glenn. I could almost see those thoughts wending through their minds.

Agent Dartle cleared her throat. "You were telling us," she said, "about any enemies Vincent Almada might have."

Glenn shook his head. "And I'm still saying I'm not the one to ask," he said, a little helplessly. "I don't know anything about his life. I don't know who he spends time with. The only reason I was the name he gave them was because Vincent knew I'd respond. That's all."

"You told them about the kidney?" I asked.

He nodded. "Yeah, yeah," he said. "But that's all it was. I mean, it's a lot, yeah, but we hardly even saw each other back then when it was happening. It didn't make us close or anything like that. We're not friends. Well, we run into each other the way everyone runs into each other in Provincetown, you know? I don't know where he lives, or anything about him other than he owns the Dolphin Fleet. He just knew I'd have to—you know—respond. Take care of getting the money. Because I owe him." He paused. "We both live in town, but we live in different worlds," he said.

Agent Nuñez frowned. "Can you explain that?"

Glenn glanced my way. I said, "I'll take this. The local history is layered, Special Agent. First were the Wampanoag Indians. Then there were English settlers, who morphed into Yankee ship captains. The town became a whaling capital. Some of the people they got to crew the whalers came from the Azores, and eventually a lot more Portuguese came here from the Azores, extended families and all that, and then when the whaling declined, the fishing took its place. After that, the artists and the bohemians came. Then it kind of morphed—again—into a gay destination, probably because the artists and writers were all such free spirits, it was welcoming." I was losing them with my little history lesson. "The point is, what Glenn is talking about, is with some exceptions, whoever lives here now belongs to those same strata, and stays in them." I could rattle it off fluently; it was a summary I often gave couples looking into a Provincetown destination wedding. We're one hell of a destination. "Vincent Almada is from an established Portuguese family, goes to Saint Peter's every Sunday, is in the Knights of Columbus, still speaks Portuguese with his parents. Glenn moved here fulltime about six or seven years ago and is gay. If it hadn't been for the kidney thing, they wouldn't have even ever met each other."

"Yet Vincent Almada asked for you to be informed." Rosa was speaking to Glenn, trying hard to pretend I wasn't part of the conversation.

"Because I owe him," said Glenn. "He knew I'd do anything to help."

"Not just you, though," said Rosa. "The message was for his wife, too." She glanced at the notebook she'd been holding. "Someone called Marie Almada?"

"Wait," I said. "What message? How was it delivered?"

James looked at me impassively. "By email," he said. "From a burner web account."

"With the picture of Vincent," added Glenn.

"Directly to Detective Agassi," added Rosa.

Well, that made sense. The chief of police was concerned with the town, town policing, town politics; Julie was the one who liaised with the state police every time we had a murder. Someone knew she was good at this stuff, even though often legally she had to take a backseat to the Staties. "Can I see it?" I asked.

"That's confidential," said James.

"Here you go," said Glenn, sounding weary. He turned his laptop around on the desk so I could see what was on it. I got up and leaned over.

An email from a Google address I didn't recognize. The message was terse—and clear.

If you want to see the owner of the Dolphin Fleet alive again, we'll need a show of good faith. Get Glenn Rogers to put $800,000 in a gym bag and give it to Marie Almada. She'll get directions for what to do with it on Friday. Bring in all the cops you want. Here's what Vinnie has to say.

The photograph showed Vincent Almada sitting in a chair. He was gagged and was holding a newspaper with yesterday's date on it in one hand and a single sheet of paper in the other. The paper had one word: *Help.*

I glanced up. "If what I've heard about him's right, he'll hate being called Vinnie."

Rosa snorted. "That's all you have to say?"

"What do you want me to say?" I straightened up and looked at her. "You're the experts, not me. He has a reputation for formality, is all. So maybe it means whoever took him doesn't know him very well. Or maybe they're trying to diminish him, using that name. I don't know. Like I said, you're the experts here."

Glenn said to me, "They haven't found Marie yet."

His wife? "Haven't found her? What does that mean?"

James flipped a hand dismissively. "She's a pilot with Cape Air. She got the message in Saint Louis. She's supposed to fly back this morning."

"And?"

"And she isn't answering her phone. And wasn't on the first flight in. There could be a lot of reasons for that. There's no need to panic."

I exchanged looks with Glenn. I didn't know Marie Almada from the grocer's daughter, but if she was anything true to form, she'd be consulting with extended family members before saying anything to the police, much less federal agents. "Well, she's not getting those instructions until tomorrow," I said cautiously. "Maybe she needs a little time to get used to the idea her husband's been kidnapped." Though I couldn't imagine not moving heaven and earth to rush back if someone had taken Ali.

"I'm sure that's it," said Rosa. She might have been a little more condescending if she'd tried. Maybe.

I asked Glenn, "What about the ransom?"

"We're handling that," snapped James. "The fewer people know about it, the better."

"Sydney has my full confidence," said Glenn.

"And I'm sure that means a lot, but not to us. We have to insist on discretion."

I shrugged. "Fine," I said. My presence wasn't accomplishing anything, I was clearly irritating them, and I had other problems to solve. "Glenn, I'll see you. Special agents, it was nice meeting you; I probably won't see you again, so—"

"They're staying at the inn," said Glenn, his voice flat. I stared at him.

Now *that* was special.

***

I went to find Mirela.

Provincetown isn't that big, we all run into everyone else, and I wanted to talk to her before she ran into Guy Husband. Who was also staying at the inn. Guy, my parents, federal agents. Damn. Just one big, happy family.

I'd told Ali he should tell Mirela about Guy, but on reflection, never mind. I didn't think it could wait a day. Someone, somewhere, was going to see him, even if she herself didn't, and then she'd hear it second- or third-hand; not good. It was just too big a risk to take.

She was in her studio, working.

Mirela's relationship to her art is a little like that of a medium to the spirit world. She waits until something insists on coming out, and then she'll stay up for three nights in a row, painting furiously. Sometimes beautiful pieces emerge. Sometimes some very weird and scary things.

"Sunshine! You know what I say when they tell me it is going to be eighty-five degrees in June?"

"You tell them what to do with their forecast?"

Her face broke into a grin, and I had to smile back. Mirela is one of the most beautiful women in the world. Blonde hair, blue eyes, a distinctive Eastern European edginess. At the moment the hair was tied back untidily with a bandana, there were flecks of paint on her cheek and forehead, and she was wearing an old paint-soaked t-shirt and painter's pants—

and she still looked better than I do after half an hour doing makeup.

I moved over to look at her current canvas. When she first came to P'town, Mirela created sedate fishing scenes, which over the past few years had devolved—or perhaps evolved—into something much more abstract, much more intuitive. "What are you working on?"

She stood back and narrowed her eyes, looking at the canvas. "I think it is about politics, sunshine, but I do not know whose."

Fair enough. "Where's Lily?"

"She has the nanny, you do not remember?"

"No, oddly enough, I don't have Lily's schedule taped to my refrigerator."

"Now you are being contrary. I think I need more depth… here," and she slashed at it with her brush.

I took some rags off one of the stools and perched on it. "Ali's coming for the weekend," I said.

That got the smile, immediate and genuine. "Oh! Such good news, sunshine. I have so much to say to him! But—your parents—they are still here?"

"They are still here." Odd when you're talking to someone who doesn't use contractions, you stop using them yourself. "I sent them out on Art's Dune Tours."

She nodded. "You needed some time away from your mother, I am thinking."

Well, that and a few other things… "Mirela, let me ask you a question. Um… this is tricky." I took a deep breath. "So… do you ever think about Guy? Guy Husband?"

There was a long pause. "About whom?" Her voice had turned frosty.

"Oh, don't do that," I said. "I know it was awful and all that, but it was a long time ago. I know you've gotten over him." Well, I thought so, anyway. "But what I want to know is, do you ever even think of him now?"

"I think of him," she said stiffly, "as much as he thinks of me."

I took a deep breath. "Then maybe I have a surprise for you," I said. "Mirela, um, there's no easy way to say this, so I'm just going to tell you. He's at the inn. Right now."

She froze, her arm reaching for the canvas. The paintbrush fell from her hand. "No."

"There's more to it," I said. "And really, all you have to do is listen, and if you don't like what you hear, I'll tell him to go away, I promise. But you just have to listen, first."

She shook her head. "I do not ever have to listen to what I do not want to hear."

I followed that one—well, at a distance, anyway. "Mirela, be quiet, okay? I'm going to tell you anyway. It wasn't really his fault he disappeared like that on you. He'd planned to do business in the city and then to come back. That's what he meant to do. But then afterward—well, he—he's been away." She started to say something and I rushed on. "I mean, of course he's been away, but what I mean is he's been *away*, away. He was in prison."

That got a reaction. She turned to me, her eyes widening. "In prison?"

I nodded. "He got involved with some complicated business deal, and the partner turned out to be shady. It happened before he came here, before—oh, before everything, the *Mignonette* and the *Bessie G* and... and you." I remembered that winter well. Ali had been undercover somewhere out on the West Coast and completely out of touch. I didn't know if he was alive or dead, in danger, being tortured, and of course I imagined the worst, all the time. And I missed him like I never thought I could miss anybody. And one night at the lighting of the lobster-pot tree I'd watched Mirela and Guy together and had felt absurdly jealous of their obvious happiness. "You know he went to New York."

She nodded. "It was the plan. He had business, then he was going to come back with his airplane and take me with him. We were meant to be together in New York for the New Year celebration." She was speaking slowly, as if she were counting. Or maybe remembering.

"Yes, well, he never got a chance. As soon as he landed in New York, right at the airport, they arrested him. And sent him home. To England. There was a trial and he went in for fifteen months."

Mirela didn't say anything, and I could see her reviewing her experience of the time. "He did not tell me."

She'd unerringly zeroed in on the real problem, of course; why? Why hadn't he contacted her, to tell her he was alive, to tell her he hadn't run out on her? It was inexplicable, and so I didn't try to explain it. "I know," I said.

"I thought he was perhaps dead."

"I know."

"I thought he was perhaps married."

"I know." I'd been with her through all these steps. Even Ali, back safe and sound from his undercover gig, even Ali hadn't been able to find him, and he looked more than was strictly within his law-enforcement purview.

Now it was clear why: because, of course, Guy hadn't been in the United States.

"Why is he here?"

I swallowed. "He says it's because he wants to see you. Because he still loves you."

She shook her head. "No. I cannot."

I nodded. It was what I'd been expecting. "Your choice. I just wanted you to know, the—the option is there. And also warn you, because you might run into him." I knew she'd want to talk once Ali got there; she always shared her thoughts with Ali. I wasn't going to push it.

"I have daughter now. I have to take care of her."

I didn't mention "taking care" of Lily was the least of the problem's Guy's resurrection presented. Between the two of them, Mirela and Guy wouldn't have any troubles; Mirela was in a way, way higher tax bracket than I was, and Guy's was in the stratosphere. But: none of my business. I didn't say anything.

Mirela retrieved her brush from the floor and stuck it, rather violently, into a jar of murky liquid. She muttered something under her breath that was, presumably, in Bulgarian. She paced over to the window and looked down on Commercial Street, the abruptly turned back to me. "How does he seem?" She looked mildly surprised at herself for asking the question.

I thought about it for a moment. "Anxious," I said finally. "I mean, anxious about you. I think he's scared you won't see him, you won't let him explain."

"You have already explained. Why should I maybe need him to explain too?"

"Well, there's that," I admitted. "Maybe it's just to assuage his conscience, I don't know. But, again, it's not me, I don't know, but perhaps you should think about it."

"Yes? This is what you would do?"

"I just said it's not me. I don't know." I shrugged. "Okay, the truth is, I have no idea what I'd do, in your place," I said frankly. "But it's been an open question for so long… and it was so painful for such a long time… well, Mirela, at least you'd have the answer. And it's no good me telling you, you know it and I know it. If you don't see him, you'll always wonder if you should have." I smiled. "At least you'll have the chance to tell him what you think of him. You can even make him grovel a little if you want."

"And that will make me feel better?"

"It would me," I said cheerfully. "But then again, I'm not as nice as you are."

"Do not believe that, sunshine. I wanted to take a dagger to his heart."

Well, now, *there* was an image that wasn't going away anytime soon. "Right," I said. "That, too. Just think about it, Mirela."

She frowned. "You are being very understanding, sunshine. It is not like you."

"Yeah, Ali said that, too. He accused me of developing empathy."

"That would be a terrible thing," she said solemnly.

***

I stopped by Big Vin's on Commercial Street to pick up a bottle of Côtes du Rhône. I had a feeling I was going to need something in my blood besides blood before the day was out. I was just making a two-dollar-difference decision when someone handed me a bottle. "Try this. You'll like it better, I promise you."

"Oh, no," I said. It was Guy Husband.

"Truly," he insisted. "It's in the same general family as your choice, but a far superior wine."

I glanced down at the bottle. "Of course it is," I snapped. "I just don't operate on a Châteauneuf-du-Pape budget."

"Then you must allow me to make a gift of it," he said smoothly.

"That sounds like bribery. And anyway, I don't even know if I should be talking to you."

"And yet here we are."

I scowled at the bottle, and then at him. "Only by accident. Have you been following me?"

"Not a bit of it. I was here already." He lifted his other hand, in which he had a bottle of Rémy Martin. "Just an accoutrement for my room at the inn," he said. "I prefer this to the brands your room service offers."

"All right." I handed the wine back to him. "Knock yourself out. I *can* be bought."

"Splendid." We moved toward the checkout counter at the front of the shop. "Have you had an opportunity to see Mirela?"

"I *made* an opportunity to see Mirela," I said. "I had to. Here you are, wandering around town without appropriate adult supervision, I couldn't have her just run into you accidentally, like I just did."

"Indeed not." He handed a credit card to the clerk. "And?"

"And nothing. She doesn't want to see you."

"Is that what she said?"

I shrugged. "More or less."

"Well, which is it? More, or less?"

"Oh, for heaven's sake." We emerged onto the street and began walking east toward the inn. "Guy, for whatever good reason you had, and I have to confess being in jail is a damned good reason for not turning up, but anyway, the reality is you *weren't* here for a few chapters, and they were kind of important ones. Maybe the most important ones." I took a breath; I'd been talking too fast. "Mirela has a baby."

That stopped him. "What? When?"

"Don't start doing arithmetic in your head," I said irritably. "It's not yours."

"You don't know that. What if—"

I grabbed his arm and made him start walking again. "Come on. Yeah, I do know that, I'm one hundred percent on that. It's not yours. It's not even *hers*, technically speaking. I mean, she didn't give birth or anything." I was getting a little out of breath. Talking to Guy and dodging pedestrians and bicycles and the heat were all conspiring against my staying cool, calm, and collected. "What happened was, she went home to Plovdiv," I said. "Her sister was having this baby she didn't want, the father was married to someone else or something like that, and Mirela went to Bulgaria and adopted her and I was so afraid she'd just stay there because she was kind of unhappy here, partly because she was still missing you but she came back home in the end so everything's all right now and I don't want you to mess that up."

Maybe I could have taken a breath in there, but it had all come out in a rush. I could still remember the fear I'd felt, the awful certainty Mirela wouldn't come back, I'd never see her again, she'd be drawn back to her native land. I'd had more than a few horrible moments there. I tried to take a deep breath. "And she's fierce about the baby, Guy." Fierce enough that last fall she'd actually shot someone who was threatening Lily. I'd known Mirela to be assertive; I'd never until then known Mirela could be *scary*.

He'd caught on to the one bit of the burst of narrative that interested him. "She was still missing me?"

This time I was the one to stop. "Look. I'm going to persuade her to talk to you," I said. "Not because I want to play matchmaker but because I have a lot going on right now and—well, because I don't want to play matchmaker. You two need to sort this out yourselves, like grownups."

"When?"

We started walking again and were already at the inn. "Seriously, Guy! I don't know. I'll check in with her later today, okay? In the meantime I have stuff to do. Ali's coming tomorrow, and—"

He was smiling. "I remember Ali," he said. Ali had arrived back from undercover while Guy was still at the inn, back during that winter, the winter he found the pirate ship.

"And he remembers you," I said tartly. "But that's not why—"

We were in the lobby and Guy's gaze had caught someone over my shoulder. "Oh, dear," he said. "Why is the FBI here?"

I glanced over and saw Glenn's two special agents conferring in the doorway to the lounge. "There's been some trouble," I said.

"I did twig onto that," he agreed. "I didn't imagine they were here on holiday."

I narrowed my eyes. "How do you know them, anyway? I thought your brushes with the law were all in England."

"I am a man of international repute," he said, but the words were automatic; I could practically feel his brain fizzing. "What's the trouble?"

"And I should tell you—why?" I countered.

"Because," Guy said, "I just might be able to help."

I glanced back at James and Rosa. She sent me a particularly nasty look. "Oh, hell, why not," I said to Guy. "Let's go get some lunch."

6

Adrienne the diva chef doesn't do lunches, except for special occasions; dinner service is her domain. But the inn's restaurant maintains her high standards all day, starting with Angus the pastry chef who arrives at three o'clock in the morning to begin the baking, through Jessie the new lunch service chef—she'd trained with Gordon Ramsay, which I suppose was a testament to her equanimity as well as her talent and work ethic—and on into tea service and finally to dinner.

It was early, so the restaurant wasn't crowded. Martin the evening maître d' was sitting at one table, inscribing the evening's specials in his fine calligraphy on the board. A family of four was arguing about someone called Jacques off in one corner, and two tables had male couples at them. I secured a table as far from the window as possible, went back to the kitchen to put in an order for *pan bagnat* for both of us without consulting Guy, and finally sat down.

He'd ordered a dry Riesling while I was occupied with the food, and one of the Handsome Young Men uncorked and poured it, smiling fetchingly at Guy all the while. Well, okay, with his casual aristocratic elegance, Guy did look like he could go either way, romantically speaking. I frowned at the waiter and he took the hint and left.

"So," Guy said as I sipped, "tell me why you're so upset and why there are FBI agents at the inn. And you may as well tell me everything, Sydney, because you know I'll find out on my own otherwise."

He did have a way of making things happen. Look what I'd done for him already today.

"You know the Dolphin Fleet?" I asked. "The people who run the whale watches off MacMillan Pier?" They hadn't been there the last time Guy had been in town; no one watches whales in the Atlantic in the winter.

He regarded me over his glass. "Take it as read," he said.

"So years and years ago there was this guy, Al Avellar, who took tourists out sports fishing in the season," I said. "And a lot of them were really impressed when they saw whales. And since whales are migrating over the shoulder seasons, in the spring and in the fall, taking people out on purpose just to watch whales seemed like a good way to extend his business. And that became the Dolphin Fleet."

"So why is the FBI interested in the Dolphin Fleet? Were they caught doing something they shouldn't?"

I shrugged. "Maybe. I don't know. But that's not what this is about. The Avellars ran it for a while—well, decades, I think. And then they sold it off to a guy called Vincent Almada, who was actually some kind of relative, which kept it all in the family, sort of."

Our lunches arrived. Guy looked a little horrified at his. "Napkins not optional," I said with a smile. "Anyway, he's been kidnapped."

"What? Who?"

"Vincent Almada. Someone's holding him and they want money to return him." I managed a bite of sandwich. If you can call it a sandwich.

"Who's holding him?"

"I think if we knew we wouldn't all be standing around doing a lot of nothing." At least, that's what the FBI looked to me to be doing. Who knew, maybe their brains were busy thinking. It couldn't hurt. "So that's why the FBI is here. I mean, they're here, specifically, because Glenn—did you meet Glenn?" He nodded, his mouth full. I went on, "So years and years ago, before Glenn was even living here, he was still in Chicago, but coming here all the time, you know, because of Barry who used to own the inn, they were partners, anyway Glenn got sick and needed a transplant. And Barry put out this panicked SOS to the community and somehow it turned out Glenn got matched up with Vincent. Or viceversa, however that works. And Glenn got one of Vincent's kidneys. And they've never even set eyes on each other since then, but now Vincent apparently told whoever has him it's Glenn who will pay." Well, maybe. The notice had come through Julie, through the Provincetown police department, which didn't sound like any kidnapping I'd ever heard of.

Not that my experience with kidnappers was that extensive. Just the one...

Guy interrupted my thoughts. "How much?"

"How much what?"

He sighed with some exaggeration, wanting me on his wavelength. "How much money are they asking for, Sydney? What's the ransom?"

"Oh. Um, eight hundred thousand."

He frowned. "Why so low?"

"So *low*? Is that what you said?"

He shook his head. "It's a lot of risk for not a lot of money, when you come down to it. The law treats kidnappings on the same level as killings. Because the danger of one leading to the other is so high, you see."

I said, sourly, "If that was meant to reassure and comfort me, it didn't quite work."

"Sydney, there are *condos* in Provincetown that cost three, four, even five times as much as that ransom demand."

Well, I knew that, but I didn't know *he* knew that. And I hadn't put it in quite that context, either. "So what are you saying?"

He didn't answer. Another bite, another swallow of wine. "Any ideas about where he's being held? Or who's holding him?"

I shook my head. I was still trying to figure out the money thing. "The FBI didn't exactly take me into their confidence," I said. "In fact, if I didn't know better, I'd say they didn't like me at all."

"Difficult as it is to imagine," said Guy.

"Right? Now, stop flirting with me," I said, and put more food in my mouth.

"In any case," said Guy, "that's a clue. They don't think as big as they think they do."

I parsed that and shook my head. "The FBI is doing the money thing with Glenn," I said.

"But you're still involved?"

I gave him a look. "Purely as an amateur," I said. "I told you, they're not really impressed with me."

"Then let's show them they're wrong."

I took a deep breath. "Guy," I said, "forgive me, but what's all this to you? I mean, yeah, thanks, but—well, you just got out of prison. Don't you have better things to do? Getting your life started again, instead of solving somebody else's problems?"

He didn't answer at first, and if I were in fact gaining some empathy in life I'd swear he was fighting some emotion. I still have to fine-tune that new ability. At last he said, "I cannot do anything until I've seen Mirela. She—the thought of her—you don't understand. Remembering her, going over our time together in my head, it's what's kept me sane for the past year. Just thinking of her. It got me through—well, I won't disturb you with the details. Let's just take it as read that she got me through everything. And if she never wishes to see me again, now, out here, in the real world, well—so be it. I won't make anything difficult. I won't stalk her and I won't contact her again. But I have to know." He took a sip of wine, slowly, thoughtfully, then set the glass down again. "As for the rest of it, Sydney, as long as I'm here waiting for Mirela, I can help you. You see, I truly don't want to pressure her. I am going to give it a week. I'll leave after that if she still won't see me. But I might as well be useful in the meantime."

"But a week is a lot of time to take off from your life," I said.

He smiled, but there wasn't anything warm about the smile, and I actually shivered. "Fifteen months is a lot of time to take off from my life," he said. "A week is nothing."

"Plus, it's easier to move things forward when you have minions who've been running your company for you anyway," I said.

Guy smiled, and this time there was humor behind it. "Plus, I have minions who've been running my company for me anyway," he agreed.

"All right," I said. "Just so we know where we stand. But your nice offer notwithstanding, I'm still not sure how you can help."

"You have to ask the right questions," he said immediately. "You have to ask who would target Vincent, and especially who would target him for such a paltry sum. Eight hundred thousand dollars? For that kind of money, it's not someone who's in it to make a fortune. It must be something personal. So, who had a personal grudge against him?"

"Okay," I said, though eight hundred thousand dollars wasn't a sum I'd have classified as paltry. "Maybe it's someone he hurt," I said, thinking it through. "Someone he offended. I don't know." I didn't know much of anything about Vincent's life, and if the answer was there, I was going to have to find someone who did. I started running through a list of Portuguese people I knew. It would have to be someone Portuguese.

There was something there, just at the edge of my consciousness. We kept thinking Portuguese... and the annual Portuguese Festival was right around the corner. Sort of. In two weeks. They'd already started putting up the flags across Commercial Street, making the rooster paintings on the sidewalks. Did that have anything to do with the kidnapping? Was it a coincidence or a plan?

Guy was on a different tangent. "The Dolphin Fleet—is it lucrative?" he asked.

I shrugged. "I'd guess so, yeah. All the trips sell out, all summer. They have a pretty steady crew, naturalists from the Center for Coastal Studies here in town, kids working the galley year after year. I can't say for sure, I don't know anything about their costs or anything like that, but it looks pretty damned lucrative to me."

"Do you know what he paid the owner— what was his name? Al something?"

"Avellar," I said. There were still Avellars in Provincetown. "And no, I don't have a clue. They're related, though, so there was probably some kind of deal."

"Anyone else interested at the time?"

"I don't know. I wasn't here. Is it important?"

Guy made a so-so gesture with his hand. "Could be. Something to think about," he said.

I frowned. "You're going somewhere with this," I said. "What exactly *are* you thinking?"

He took another deep breath. "I might be totally wrong," he said. "But here it is. When I was applying for my permits for the search for the *Mignonette*, I learned something about the politics around here. And they can get more than a little ruthless."

I had to laugh. "You're kidding, right? This is *Provincetown*, Guy! We don't do ruthless here." I paused, thinking. "Well, not when it matters, anyway."

He finished his lunch and pushed the plate away. "Not Provincetown," he said. "I'm not talking about Provincetown. I'm talking about New Bedford."

New *Bedford*? Where had that come from? It was a rough hard-working port city on the south coast of Massachusetts with a significant Portuguese population. Putting New Bedford into the mix did up the ante a notch… or five. "But that's *fishing*," I said slowly. "Not tourist stuff like a whale watch."

"You've never heard of diversifying a business?"

I thought about it for a moment. New Bedford. Holy shit. That really could bring it to a whole new level. I knew some of the guys who worked for the harbormaster, and I even knew a couple of the local commercial fishermen, and they all had the same story about the New Bedford crews.

Poaching. Big—really big—commercial rigs out of New Bedford, scalloping right off Herring Cove—which was pretty much raising a middle finger to the P'town commercial fleet; I'd seen one or two of them myself when I was out "doing sunset," as we called it. Right off the beach. Every time it happened, Provincetown complained, and New Bedford did—well, whatever they did, maybe a fine, who knew? And the boats—some of them really high-tech combination dragger and scallopers, big, state-of-the-art rigs—just kept coming. New Bedford has been the largest producer of sea scallops in the States for decades. It was easy to see why.

What I didn't see was how Guy knew about it, and why, and what that meant. "So they poach," I said, half-shrugging. "They're still the six-hundred-pound gorilla on the East Coast. They're sure not hurting, not like the Cape Cod fleet is." Which made the poaching all the more unfair, the subject of many drunken conversations down at the Old Colony or the Governor Bradford. New Bedford had everything, and still took from us. "Why diversify now?"

There was a short pause. They've been selling off the Lima vessels and permits," said Guy, and waited for that to sink in.

It did, slowly. Marcos Lima, locally and colloquially known as the Codfather, had over a number of years put together a massive fishing empire out of New Bedford, with a whole fleet of boats he owned—in one way or another. There were other players, but he was the only one that mattered.

He hadn't come by his empire honestly, though: when he caught any fish subject to strict catch limits, like gray sole or cod, he'd report his nets filled with something plentiful, like haddock. He'd written the book: Overfishing For Fun and Profit.

He was this larger-than-life figure on the city's waterfront, totally owned the docks, terrorized any potential competition, and once boasted his deals worked as a regular money laundromat. Unfortunately for him, the people he said that to were IRS agents posing as Russian entrepreneurs, and thirty years after it started, the scheme collapsed. Lima went to prison and now, apparently, his assets were being sold off. "The Codfather's in jail," I said to Guy. "He can't be behind this."

He put his elbows on the table and leaned in. "First of all," he said, "believe me when I tell you, being imprisoned does not necessarily—or even probably—reduce one's outside influence and business dealings. Nothing changes for some of these chaps. I've seen it first-hand now myself." Yeah, I thought, and no doubt participated.

While you were busy not contacting Mirela. That was still stinging.

"Secondly," Guy continued, "we're talking about something that happened in the past. When did this Avellar character sell the Dolphin fleet to his cousin?"

"I have no idea," I admitted.

"Chances are, it was when Lima was at the height of his business," said Guy. "Look, it's less of a long shot than you may be thinking. You just have to think beyond Provincetown.

I know for a *fact* he was looking to get a foot-hold into *my* business, marine exploration and salvage, which is a *great* deal less of a sure thing than a whale-watch outfit. I'll just say the attempt wasn't precisely following law-abiding or ethical channels, and leave it at that."

There was a story there, I thought, but didn't interrupt him. "I'm simply saying the New Bedford mob play rough. I wouldn't put it past them to use whatever tactics they can make work to get what they want. And the low sticker price on this Vincent chap, that's really the tell, isn't it? That's what clued me in there's something more afoot. These are people who rake in millions of unreported income every year and are always, *always* looking for their main chance. There's never too much of anything for them. Perhaps there's not even ever enough of anything." He took a breath and looked at me. "What I'm saying is perhaps they still want the Dolphin Fleet."

"But why now?" I asked. "Whenever it was, whatever happened back then, that transaction between Vincent and the Avellars was years and years ago. This doesn't make sense. Why kidnap Vincent *now?*"

Guy leaned back and put his napkin on the table. "Because everything's changed since then," he said. "This is the absolute correct time to do it. What I didn't tell you is this: part of Lima's deal, along with the jail time he is required to serve, is complete forfeiture of anything attached in any way to commercial fishing. He can never fish again, he cannot own interest in anything involved with fishing, and he knows they'll be scrutinizing his every move once he's out. Well, actually, he knows they're scrutinizing his moves *now*. And what that means is, it's time to start something new. And start it somewhere else, close enough to keep an eye on, far enough away for deniability."

"A whale watch," I said. It just could make sense.

He shrugged. "It's not necessarily true. I'm just telling you one possible scenario," he said. "I may be completely off base here, and I'd be glad if that were the case. Because I have to tell you, if it's the New Bedford mob…"

"Yes?"

"Then, well, let's hope the FBI know what they're doing," he said soberly. "Or Vincent Almada could end up as a corpse."

7

And then, of course, he did.

We didn't know about it right away. The FBI was doing whatever the FBI did, Julie was doing whatever the police did, Glenn had secured financing and was preparing the requested (and classic, you had to admit) gym bag in which to place the unmarked bills, Guy was staying away from Mirela, and I was dealing with my parents, fresh off their dune tour and clambake.

"We saw more whales from the beach," my mother reported. "Our driver, such a nice young man, and not even married, can you imagine? He gave us binoculars. His name was Allen. Or Andrew. They were humpbacks," she added, nodding knowingly.

My mother, the cetacean expert.

"Even your father was impressed," she said. "Isn't that right, Edward?"

"They were excellent binoculars," he told me. "I'm ordering myself a pair online. They're image-stabilized. The clarity was stunning."

"Well, good, then," I said, a little uncertainly. I had no idea what he was talking about. But at least they'd had a good time. I couldn't wait to see the bill I'd get from Rob.

Maybe I could get Guy to pay it. After all, it had kept them out of *his* hair, too.

Because of course they knew each other: my parents had arrived for a Christmas visit the year while Guy was still in town, and my mother had absolutely adored him. Having my mother adore you is almost as bad as having her despise you: either way, you're in for far more attention than you want. Guy was fortunate my mother hadn't attached herself to him like a leech. Not yet, anyway.

"Did you get your work finished?" my mother demanded. "We were hoping you'd spend maybe just a *little* time with us while we're here."

"Something's come up," I said, and put up my hand to stop her immediate reaction. "But I promise it won't interfere with dinner, don't worry. And Ali's coming in on the ferry tomorrow, staying for the weekend." I watched while my mother absorbed this information.

"He's, um, looking forward to seeing you again."

She hadn't yet decided how she wanted to respond to this turn of events, so she chose instead to ignore it. "Well! I'm going up to the room to rest. We've been out in the sun all this time, and I'm tired. And it's hot. Are you coming, Edward?"

My father grimaced at me behind her back. "Of course," he said, and to me, "What time is dinner?"

"Reservations at seven," I said. "Come down earlier for cocktails if you'd like."

He looked as if he'd like a couple of cocktails right then, but he just nodded and followed my mother.

"Whew," said a voice at my elbow. It was Glenn. "You're keeping them busy," he observed.

"Trying to," I said. Better than to make them relive those terrifying days when Alex disappeared, when we got the photograph and the demand letter and I had to think that she hadn't been as pretty in that picture as she'd been when she left home. I wondered, not for the first time, where my parents had been getting the money; they were well-off, but it had been far more than they could pay on their own. Not the bargain-basement price Guy insisted was being asked for Vincent.

That was all I'd ever heard about it: they were getting the money. I took a deep breath and shook off the memories. "What's new here?" I asked Glenn.

He jerked his head toward the back door and we went into the courtyard. "The money's ready," he said, his voice low. A few guests around the pool noted our presence but kept doing whatever they were doing. "And Marie Almada's just gotten in. Nuñez and Dartle went to the airport to pick her up."

I noted his use of the last names. "You're not finding the agents all that special, then?"

He rolled his eyes. "They'll handle her with the delicacy of a steam roller." He paused, and I wondered if his mind was going where mine was, to the day I'd picked him up at Provincetown's tiny airport and he'd been expecting nothing more than a month in the sun with his beloved partner Barry. Instead, I'd been the one to tell him Barry was dead.

I roused myself. "Probably," I agreed. "Nothing we can do about that. Will they take her home?"

"I doubt it," he said gloomily. "The whole circus seems to be happening here. P'town police are at the house, and I don't think the FBI enjoy playing in the same sandbox. Or maybe the police know something the rest of us don't."

"What on earth?"

"Who knows? Julie Agassi moves in mysterious ways."

Indeed. "Do you know her? Vincent's wife? Marie Almada?"

He shook his head. "Never met her. Just what we need, her getting all hysterical in the lobby. I suppose we'll have to find *her* a room, too, with the house taped off as a possible crime scene." He looked at me accusingly. "Mike should be here to handle all this," he complained.

"You're the one sent him on sabbatical, not me," I said, raising my hands in denial. "Me, I'd never let him out of my sight if I were you." Mike is super-efficient; I'd keep him chained to the inn if I were Glenn.

He narrowed his eyes. "And what about you? Aren't you supposed to be doing weddings, or something?"

"Well, something, anyway." I caught his expression and relented. "It's all good, Glenn, don't worry. There's a wedding Sunday afternoon and everything's in place for it. The cake, the music, the officiant, everything. Then there are two more next week and they're good, too." Or would be, once I made just a *few* more phone calls...

"Okay." He stared at the pool and the tiki bar beyond it without really seeing anything.

"I hope they can pull this off," he said. His voice tightened. "The guy saved my life, Sydney."

I touched his arm, briefly. "I know," I said gently. "Everyone's doing everything they can."

"I know." But there were lines around his eyes and even his beard looked somehow wilder than usual, more unkempt. Glenn was right: he really needed Mike there to run things.

The kid from Reception was in the doorway and spotted Glenn. "Boss?"

He took a deep breath and turned to face him. "What is it, Jack?"

"Someone here to see you," he said. "Says it can't wait." He hesitated. "It's the police," he added, in a suitably lowered voice.

"Just what we need," said Glenn, and looked at me. "You coming?"

"Aye, aye, captain," I said, "Lead on."

Julie Agassi was at Reception, looking very official in her uniform and examining one of the inn's brochures. "I didn't know you have a hot tub here," she remarked.

"Over in the spa," said Glenn. "What is it?"

She put the brochure down and straightened. "Vincent Almada," she said. "He washed up under MacMillan Wharf."

I swallowed. "Washed up… as in…?"

"Dead," she confirmed with a nod. "Dead in the water. One of the squid jiggers found him."

Glenn was looking dazed. "But he can't be," he said. "I *said* I'd get the money. And I did." I was having a severe case of *déja vu*. Glenn looked at me. "I did," he repeated. "I was doing what they want. I have the bag in my office. I was waiting for them to call—they said they'd call tonight. It isn't time yet. He can't be dead."

I could hear Guy's voice, over lunch, pointing out the low sticker price they'd been asking for Vincent. "They never meant to let him go," I said.

Julie looked interested. "You know this how?"

"Oh, hell. Do we really have to have this conversation here?" Glenn demanded.

"Come on," I said firmly. Someone had to take charge, and these two were among the most take-charge people I knew; it was more than a little scary to be the only one here who had her act together. I went into the private lounge and they followed.

There were a couple of guys there discussing some drag show over at the Pilgrim House. "And what a hoot! She gets more daring every year, I swear she does."

"You have to leave," I informed them. "Sorry, but we need the room."

One of them looked as if he might be about to say something to me, then caught sight of Julie's uniform over my shoulder. "Sure, sure," he muttered as they decamped.

I shut the door and leaned against it. "Guy Husband is in town," I said.

"I know," said Glenn.

"What does that have to do with anything?" Julie wanted to know.

"He knows—knew—about the kidnapping," I said. "Okay, sorry, mea culpa, I'm the one who told him. But he'd guessed something was up. He's no idiot. And he said the ransom price was way too low for the risk involved." I paused, but nobody said anything. Julie was looking at me as though I were some new fashion she wasn't sure would catch on. "He suggested it might have been Vincent's competition for the Dolphin Fleet."

"Vincent had no competition for the Dolphin Fleet," said Julie, shaking her head. "It was all arranged in advance. It was always going to Vincent."

"Wait," said Glenn. "Just Vincent? Not Vincent and Marie?"

Something that might have been amusement flitted briefly across Julie's face. "I see you haven't met Marie," she said. Glenn shook his head. She made a face. "Let's just say she wasn't interested in any business venture with her husband," she said.

"She's on her way here now," Glenn pointed out. "Like everyone else on the planet, apparently." He caught her expression. "Why? What should I know?"

"You'll know everything soon enough," she said obscurely, and turned back to me. "What other pearls of wisdom did Guy Husband have to share? What made him think there was competition for the fleet?"

"Just that the New Bedford crew had tried to muscle in on his operation here, remember, winter before last? And he thinks with the loss of the fishing permits they're looking for expansion opportunities," I said.

"*Lima's* people?" Julie sounded incredulous. "That's reaching, Sydney."

I shrugged, which was really uncomfortable up against the door. "Ow. But there had to be a reason they didn't ask for much ransom, I mean apparently in the greater scheme of things they didn't really ask for much, and there had to be a reason they killed him. How did he die, anyway?"

"Pathologist's on his way from Sandwich," she said. "Looks like a drowning."

Poor squid jiggers, I thought, and then, never mind the squid jiggers: poor dead Vincent.

There was the sound of shouting out in the lobby, a strident female voice and a couple of others responding.

"Ah," said Julie. "I hear Marie Almada has arrived."

***

She had indeed.

Portuguese women are strong, strong as the men who haul the catch, strong as the storms that batter the coast. Generations of them cooked the food, made the clothes, raised the kids, handled emergencies while their fathers and husbands and brothers and sons were out on extended fishing trips, sometimes for months. They got good at waiting. They got good at waiting long past when the boats were due back. They yelled at their kids and grandkids and spent frugally and said the rosaries at daily Mass, as though daring God to defy them. Women of steel.

If most Portuguese women were made of steel, Marie Almada was titanium. Sleek, modern, and inflexible.

We emerged from the private lounge to something of a scene in reception. Special

Agent James Nuñez was trying to maintain the upper hand, and it wasn't even close to working. "We need you to—"

"What do you mean, I can't go home? What the *hell* am I doing here?"

"We need you to answer—"

"I'm not answering shit until you tell me what's going on!"

Marie Almada was of medium height, black hair pulled back into some sort of bun that was coming undone, and wearing her Cape Air captain's uniform. With most pilots, you meet the uniform first. With Marie, it was the voice. She caught sight of Julie and went off. "I suppose this is your idea, *Detective* Agassi, and you can just forget it! What the hell is going on? I'm not talking to anybody until I get some questions answered!"

Rosa Dartle put a placating hand on Marie's arm and Marie shook it off so hard she probably bruised it. "Don't touch me!"

Behind me, Glenn said, unhappily, "We need to take this somewhere else."

Jack, the Handsome Young Man at Reception, had his mouth hanging open in horror. Several guests were edging carefully out of the room, and a few curious onlookers were peering in the front door. Not exactly great public relations for the Race Point Inn.

Julie stepped forward. "Marie," she said, in that pitched-louder-than-normal voice that cops and emergency workers use when they're figuring out what's going on.

"Oh, so *now* you notice me. What about when I was complaining about that fool parking his truck in our yard last fall? You weren't quite so accommodating then, *detective!*"

"Marie," Julie said calmly, "You set that truck on *fire.*" Glenn and I exchanged startled looks.

"You weren't doing anything about it, what was I supposed to do?" There had to be a calm side to this woman, I found myself thinking, otherwise Cape Air wouldn't put her in charge of any of their aircraft. The thought of being with her in a small plane was enough to make anyone reach for their rosary beads. Hell, the thought of being with her *anywhere*...

Julie said, "We have to talk to you, Marie. Now."

Marie had clearly already dismissed the federal agents as inconsequential, but she was paying attention, if belligerently, to Julie. "You offering me something, *detective?*"

"Come in here and talk to me," said Julie.

James Nuñez said, "Now, just a minute, we're—"

Julie cut him off. She hadn't taken her eyes off Marie. "As soon as I have a chance to talk to Mrs. Almada, you can ask her what you want." And when Rosa made a gesture toward Marie—as though possession were indeed nine-tenths of the law—Marie rounded on her. "Try that again and I'll sue you!" she spat out.

"Marie?" Julie was the picture of calm. "Can you come in here now? You're making Mr. Rogers nervous."

The name got through, as it had been meant to. Marie rounded on us and her eyes went right to Glenn. She knew him in that moment, knew who he was, remembered what had happened. That he was alive and well and living in Provincetown completely because of her husband. "Okay," she said, suddenly subdued. "But I don't want the feds in there."

"Hey—" started James, but Julie quelled him with a look. "I'm going to talk to Mrs. Almada," she said, "and *then* you can ask her whatever you want." She closed the door gently but definitively behind us.

I probably wasn't supposed to be part of this little group, but I'd drifted in and no one said anything, so I retired to the far end of the lounge and promised myself I'd stay quiet.

Like *that* was ever going to happen.

8

We've been trying to contact you," Julie said.

"Yeah, great, so now you have. What is it? What the hell's going on? Why can't I go home?"

Glenn stirred. "You might want to sit down," he said.

"I'm fine where I am." Her eyes went from him to Julie, and something in her relented. Slightly. "Tell me."

Julie said, "It's Vincent. I'm sorry to tell you he's dead."

It was exactly the right approach. I'm always put off by crime shows on TV where the cops go to do the death knock and end up with long pauses and embarrassed expressions and not meeting the person's eyes. Too much drama, not enough common sense.

Dramatic pauses weren't going to work with Marie. She did sit down on the couch, suddenly, as if her legs had given way under her, but she didn't cry out and she didn't deny what she was hearing. "When?" Her voice was perfectly steady.

"We think sometime last night," Julie answered, sitting down in the chair at right angles to the couch.

"You *think*? That's all? What happened?"

Julie took a deep breath. "Marie. He was abducted sometime yesterday. There was a ransom demand, made to Glenn, which came through the police department."

"And what? You couldn't pay?" The dark eyes were on him now.

Julie said, "That's not what happened."

"I was getting the money," Glenn said, the horror still real and alive in his voice. "I was getting it."

Marie pointed at him. "I know who you are. You're the one Vincent donated the kidney for. That's why."

Glenn said, unhappily, "Yes. I was—"

Julie cut him off. "The deadline hadn't passed, Marie. We don't know what happened. We're investigating. That's what the two federal agents in the lobby are here for."

"Those two?" Scorn in her voice. "They won't find anything. How did he die?"

"We're waiting for the medical examiner to tell us. Possibly drowning. He was in the water. We'll know more soon."

"So he was being held on a boat?" Marie, daughter and granddaughter of fishermen.

"We don't know," Julie said gently. "But we're going to tell you everything we can as soon as we can. I promise you."

My mind wandered. Where *had* Vincent been held? Wouldn't that give a clue to who'd taken him?

The boat option was obvious. This time of year, the harbor was filled with them: sailboats, motorboats, even the occasional small houseboat. Moorings from Flyer's for townspeople who did recreational boating; sailors passing through; mega-yachts, summer people—when Thea and I used to rent a 19-foot sailboat and tool around the harbor, the hardest part was navigating past all the moored boats.

A dinghy or a Zodiac rowed or motored out to any of those boats on a regular basis would arouse no suspicion at all. People came and went all the time, and the harbormasters had their hands full enough—with the more obvious transgressions as well as the constant maritime traffic—to notice anything that low-key. If the prisoner were tied and gagged, or drugged, there would be no cause for any attention.

In a place like Provincetown you'd probably be crazy to *not* keep your captive on board, come to think of it.

And it might explain Vincent's body washing up under MacMillan Pier. Maybe his captors really meant to collect the ransom, and it was simply he'd escaped, jumped overboard and swum for shore. He could easily have drowned—he came from a fishing family, and a lot of the fishermen around here don't swim; they say if you go down out in the Atlantic it's easier to just let the cold take you. The scientists call it cold-water shock: if you're suddenly immersed in frigid water, you automatically gulp the water in and your muscles become uncontrollable.

The Labrador Current is right on our doorstep, so the fishermen and the scientists are all probably right. I'd been dunked in the harbor myself and knew how close to death from hypothermia I'd come.

But that had been in October; the water was cold now, but possibly survivable. Whether or not he could swim was a different issue.

Still, there was something about the Vincent-on-a-boat scenario that bothered me, and I couldn't quite put my finger on what it was.

Maybe the proximity of the Dolphin Fleet it-self—they had five whale boats going in and out of MacMillan all day, every day, this time of year, and they might notice something spe-cific to Vincent that others could miss. Okay, that could be a little farfetched, but there was something tickling my brain, just a little out of reach…

"Do you own a boat?" I asked, suddenly, and everyone looked at me; their conversation had continued while I was wool-gathering, and I'd interrupted somebody.

Marie frowned. "And you are—who, ex-actly?"

It probably wouldn't be reassuring to her to hear I was the wedding planner. I suspected most people in my profession don't moonlight solving crimes. "I work here," I said, a little lamely. "I'm a friend of Glenn's."

Julie was giving me her standard I'm-about-to-throw-you-out-of-the-detectives'-club look. "Sydney?"

"I was just thinking," I said, "if Vincent and Marie own a boat out in the harbor, he might have been kept there. He might have gone out to it and they boarded it." My imag-ination was tripping right along now. He could even have taken it out, and they rushed him at sea, modern-day pirates. It wouldn't be the first time I'd encountered something like that…

Marie shook her head. "We don't have a boat," she said. "What do we want a boat for? What're we supposed to do with a boat?" She looked at me a little pityingly and I remembered, too late, that a lot of people who make their living on the water don't view it as recreational space. Okay, so not my brightest train of thought.

Julie didn't care about boats; she was pursuing schedules. "What would he normally be doing day before yesterday? Tuesday?" she asked.

It was her turn to get the withering stare. "How am I supposed to know what he was doing on Tuesday?" Marie demanded. "What *Vincent* was doing? Are you serious?"

"It would be helpful to know," Julie said calmly. Granted that it would take more than Marie Almada to rattle her, but there was impatience lurking behind that calm; I knew her well enough to figure that one out.

"Listen. Here's what Tuesday was. I flew into Saint Louis," Marie said. "There was an emergency at the airport and the tower kept us in the pattern for an hour and I was right up against my hours—flying overtime. I had a coffee with a friend, checked into the hotel, watched the news, and went to bed. Why would I talk to Vincent?"

Because a lot of married people would, I thought. Ali and I weren't married, and we checked in with each other daily, even if only for a few minutes, unless he was out on assignment. Sometimes even then.

And if I was thinking that, you can bet the feds were, too, and I could imagine them right outside the door, waiting impatiently to talk to Marie. Who probably inherited everything when Vincent died... including the Dolphin Fleet.

Julie wasn't going there. Not yet, anyway. "How would he typically spend a weekday?" she asked, conversationally. "Did he spend time in the office?" I didn't even know where the whale-watch office was. There was a kiosk on MacMillan Pier, but a real office? Probably there had to be one...

Marie was staring at her as though they were speaking different languages. "Vincent *owns* the fleet," she said. "He doesn't *manage* it." She sighed, loudly, throwing up her hands. "All right. Here you go. Nice days he starts out at the Café Maria. Him and his friends sit around and talk about the old days or God only knows what for an hour or God only knows how long. He takes a walk because the doctor said he has to. He goes to the market.

He sits out on the bench in front of Town Hall for a while. He reads the paper. He sits around with the guys and drinks port. They used to do it at the VFW, they go to the Governor Bradford now. Maybe he eats there if I'm not in town, maybe he cuts up come linguica and eats it with bread and cheese. If I'm here he comes home and I cook. He watches the news. He goes to bed. Maybe that's what he did on Tuesday. That good enough for you, detective?"

Not exactly, I reflected, a hands-on owner. But then I supposed he didn't have to be. And I had to admit that, even in the middle of a murder investigation, the linguica, bread, and cheese option sounded pretty good to me.

Julie wasn't giving up easily. "Marie. I'm not the enemy. We're trying to help you, here," she said softly. "We just want to find out what happened."

"Help me? You're kidding, right? My husband's dead, detective. You gonna bring him back? Your questions gonna bring him back?" She shook her head and for the first time leaned back into the couch. "No? I didn't think so. I want to take a shower. I want to arrange for my husband's funeral. Ask me what you need to ask, and just let me go home."

To whom? I realized I didn't even know if she and Vincent had children. Would that make a difference?

There seemed to be a lot here I didn't know.

Glenn said, gently, "We're sorry for your loss. It's a terrible thing to have happen. It's hard to let it really sink in. My partner was murdered a few years ago. I know what you're feeling."

Wrong thing to say. She was up off the sofa faster than I've ever seen anyone move. "You know how I feel?" she demanded. "How do you know how I feel? You don't know anything about me! You don't know anything about my life or about my marriage or about my husband! Don't you look me in the face and pretend you do!" It was the closest she'd come so far to showing grief—even if it was coming out as anger—and I was secretly relieved. Surely she didn't have anything to do with Vincent's death. This emotion was raw, and very real.

Julie was unimpressed. She sighed, stood up, put her notebook away. "You can't leave yet, Marie," she said. "The federal agents want to talk to you."

"And if I don't want to talk to them?"

"I think you'll find," said Julie, "that you don't have a choice."

***

By that time, I didn't, either.

Glenn was right: the inn had somehow become Crime Solving Central, and while my mother is great at ignoring what she doesn't want to see or hear or know, even she wasn't going to be able to stay in denial for long.

In a way—though I felt a twinge of guilt in admitting it—Vincent's death had gotten me off the hook. It was murder we were discussing now, not kidnapping. With a little luck they might not hear the echo of that giggle, catch a glimpse of the ghost as she slipped around a corner.

Or so I most fervently hoped.

I met them for a cocktail in the bar beside the restaurant. Conversation was limited due to the crush of people around us and the various conversations going on in at least two languages.

There was classical music playing softly in the restaurant. Martin the maître d' brought us to a table and held the chair out for my mother, who flirted outrageously with him in return. "Such beautiful music," she said.

"When we host special dinners, we have a string quartet," I said.

My father was anxiously scanning the menu and you could see the exact moment he relaxed. I smiled at him. "Yes," I said, "it's there." His favorite appetizer: a fig and goat cheese tartine, drizzled with local honey. I'd already checked.

We spent some time making choices about food and wine and shared them with the sommelier and the waiter, and then we were alone. I wanted to be the one to tell them so the version they got was edited. "So you'll notice a lot of things going on," I said.

"Yes, what is that about?" my mother wanted to know.

"You know the whale watch boat we were out on yesterday?" I asked her. Was it only yesterday? It felt like a month ago. "Well, the man who owns the company, the Dolphin Fleet, he was killed sometime yesterday." Well, probably.

My father looked startled. "By a whale?"

"Good heavens, no," I said quickly. "He drowned." Again, probably.

"He fell off a whale watch boat?" My mother asked. "Actually, I'm not surprised. You know, it did get crowded up by the railing there."

To the best of my knowledge, Vincent didn't actually go on any of the Dolphin Fleet excursions. As Marie said, he owned the fleet, he didn't manage it. "I don't think that's what happened, Ma."

"Oh, no," she said, and was immediately interrupted by the sommelier with the Chardonnay. We waited while my father took the ritual first sip, approved the choice, and then waited while our glasses were filled. I held up my wine. "To your vacation!"

My mother was having none of it. "Do not tell me this poor man was murdered and you're going to be part of the investigation," she said.

I sipped my wine. It was still better, I thought, than the alternative conversation we could have been having, the one about Vincent first being kidnapped. "It's not clear yet what happened," I said carefully.

My father's beloved appetizer and my own basket of gougères, lighter-than-air cheese puffs, all arrived; and no sooner had the waiter departed than someone else took his place. "I wonder," an English voice said diffidently, "if I might join you for dinner?"

Guy.

I got ready to say no, but my mother was already basking in the glow of his gaze. "Mr. Husband," she said, and I could swear it sounded like she was purring. "We'd be delighted." My father bent himself into that half-way-up shape men do when they're trying to be polite but don't feel like standing up, and I shrugged. "Do what you want to do," I said. I was being rude and I knew it; but it's harder to navigate the perils of conversation when you're not sure who's in charge of the boat.

"So good to see you again, Frances," said Guy. *He'd better not kiss her hand,* I thought. *I will be* seriously *nauseated if he kisses her hand.*

He didn't. He and my father nodded to each other and my father went back to his tartine. Guy topped off my glass—I was the only one who had touched it so far—and poured some wine for himself. I wondered if I could kick him under the table.

My mother had gone from purring to cooing. Here was someone, after all, whose last name was her favorite word, and she was nowhere close to wearing it out. "Mr. Husband," she said again, "are you in town looking for another wreck?"

Guy laughed. "No, I'm afraid not," he said. "I've come hoping to spend some time with Mirela. Seeing you is a bonus, of course."

"Of course," I said.

My mother shot me a look. "That's kind of you to say," she said to Guy. "Sydney, wasn't Mirela going to join us for dinner tonight?" She looked around vaguely, as though waiting for Mirela to materialize nearby.

"She was," I agreed. "But she decided not to." I hoped Guy was interpreting my glare correctly.

The waiter took away the appetizer plates and served our main course. Fish for the Riley contingent: coquilles saint-Jacques, sole meunière, pike quenelles with lobster sauce. Late to the party, Guy was the odd man out with lamb, but gamely ordered another two bottles of the Chardonnay.

I wished he'd go away.

"So we heard about the owner of the whale-watching outfit," said my mother. "Poor man."

"Yes," I said quickly. It was probable Guy, being Guy, had picked up the gossip around the pool or the bar and knew Vincent had gone from being a kidnap victim to a possible murder victim, but I wasn't taking any chances with him saying the wrong thing. "It's terrible that he drowned. I met his widow a little earlier."

"I rather think," said Guy, 'that the whole *inn* met his widow a little earlier." He slanted a knowing smile at me over the rim of his wineglass before taking a sip.

"What does that mean?" my mother demanded.

"Just that Mrs. Almada… has a strong personality," said Guy. "And makes no secret of it."

I suddenly resented him being there. At our table. In my town. Walking back onstage after too many acts had been played out, and behaving as if he'd never left. Talking about Marie as though he knew her; telling my parents amusing stories—as he was now—about Provincetown, as if he actually had a stake in the place.

Damn it, I wasn't even enjoying Adrienne the diva chef's sole meunière, and that was, gastronomically speaking, a cardinal sin.

"We were thinking of going on another whale watch," my mother was saying. "It was so much more fun than I'd thought it would be! Edward didn't get to go with Sydney and me, and he really wants to go."

I glanced at my father, who gave no indication of having heard anything. He was probably rehearsing what he'd say to Adrienne the diva chef about her scallops. I still couldn't quite believe such a mild-mannered man was able to go into the jaws of hell—read, Adrienne the diva chef's kitchen—and emerge unscathed. My father really did have unplumbed depths.

My mother wasn't finished. "You really must come with us, Mr. Husband. I insist. It's an extraordinary experience. Did you know humpback whales don't have teeth?"

"Guy's only here for a week, Ma," I said a little desperately.

"Well, we're only here for a few more days ourselves, so we'll do it soon," said my mother, as if that settled it.

"*And* he's seen tons of whales in his line of work anyway," I added.

That got her attention. "Are you taking a tone with me?"

"No, I'm not. I'm just saying Guy has better things to do than go on a whale watch—"

"To the contrary," said Guy, patting his mouth with his napkin before reaching over and refilling my mother's glass. "It sounds quite interesting. Check out the Dolphin Fleet. First whale-watching on the East Coast, aren't they?"

"Why yes, I do believe so. That young man told us. Or was it Mr. Rogers? What was that young man's name, Sydney? The one on the whale watch?"

"Kai," I said. "He's a scientist at the Center for Coastal Studies."

"Kai," my mother repeated. "Strange name, isn't it? I wonder where he's from?"

Before she could let her xenophobia take over, I said, "He went to Northeastern, Ma."

"Well, a lot of foreigners go to our schools, dear."

Breathe, Riley. Just breathe.

9

After dinner—and my father's inevitable and very daring visit to the kitchen to congratulate Adrienne the diva chef on another memorable meal—my parents decided on an early night. Which was just fine with me.

"What are you playing at?" Guy and I had drifted outside to the patio surrounding the pool. Some guys were in it, not swimming, just standing up to their waists and talking, occasionally dunking into the water. There was a middle-aged straight couple at the tiki bar. It was surprisingly uncrowded for June.

"What do you mean?" He was the picture of insouciance.

"Hijacking the table. Telling my mother you'll go on a whale watch."

"I won't, don't worry. But why shouldn't I go on a whale watch?"

I let out my breath in a snort. "This is ridiculous. My family has nothing to do with you. My town has nothing to do with you. Right now, *I* don't want to have anything to do with you. Maybe you didn't notice, but we've all been fine without you. You're so used to being at the center of things you can't stand it when people aren't going, *Oh, Guy, you're wonderful.*"

"Yes," he said. "I very much enjoyed being at the center of things when I was in prison."

That stopped me, as of course it was meant to. "I didn't mean—"

Guy took my arm and steered me over to one of the empty tables ranged around the pool. "Listen," he said as we sat down. "I think I can help. There's no reason for me not to."

"So you can show Mirela what a hero you are?" I yanked my arm from his grasp.

"You think the two special agents in there are going to solve this? A kidnapping and a murder?"

"We don't know it's a murder."

"Yes, we do. The police said so this afternoon."

How had he suddenly gotten in the loop? It was making my head hurt. "Anyway, yeah, I do think they're going to figure it out. That's what they do. They're the FBI, for heaven's sake." But it hadn't worked for my sister. They hadn't figured out anything about Alexandra. They'd never found out what had happened to Alexandra. I shivered involuntarily and took a deep breath. Anyway, if there was any amateur involvement here, that was *my* role. Time-tested and (nearly) Julie-approved.

Damn; was I actually *jealous* of Guy Husband? That was ridiculous. Wasn't it? "So what's your plan? Take over the investigation?"

"No; just help with it." He leaned toward me, intense, earnest. "Listen, Sydney. I've got some people in New Bedford now. They—"

"You've got people in *New Bedford*?"

He leaned back again. I have that effect on people sometimes. "The FBI aren't pursuing that option," he said reasonably. "They've got their hands full right here. In fact, no one's seeing it as an option at all, are they?"

"It's not an option, it's a theory. *Your* theory."

"Then no one will care what I do to set my own mind at rest," he said. "I'm not treading on anyone's toes."

There was an uncomfortable silence. What he was saying made sense. "You have people in New Bedford? Really?" I asked again, this time without the sarcasm.

He shrugged. "I have people anywhere I want them," he said.

Not sure I wanted to know any specifics there. There was a side to Guy that... unnerved me, somehow. Something lurking just under the elegant calm surface, like a Great

White out in the bay, just waiting for the right moment to surface and strike... I mentally shook myself. Ridiculous.

Well it was, wasn't it?

"Your people," I said carefully. "They're—they operate within the law, right?" What we didn't need was Guy bringing his legal problems along with his unexpected return. I knew rich people sometimes cut corners. I didn't want any of those corners cutting *us*.

He answered my thought and not my question. "I assure you, Sydney, nothing will happen that will come back to hurt you, or Mirela, or anyone here."

"That isn't reassuring," I said.

"It's all I can say to you now," he said blandly. "Listen, I know you think otherwise, I know you don't trust me, but I seriously mean you no harm at all. As I said before, I really simply want to help."

"And see Mirela."

"And see Mirela," he agreed, nodding.

So we were back to Square One. I sighed. "Are you really going on a whale watch?"

"I thought I might at some point. Get a feel for the whale-watch company."

"You'll get a feel for the *tourists*," I said repressively.

"Will you be going?"

"I don't see how I can get out of it," I said, and sighed again. "All right. I'll get tickets for Saturday."

"Why not tomorrow?"

"Ali's coming over from Boston tomorrow," I said, regretting the words as soon as they were out of my mouth. Damn it, for someone who had disappeared for over a year, Guy was fast making inroads again into being One of Us.

He didn't say anything for a few moments, his eyes on the guys in the pool but not, I thought, really seeing them. Finally he seemed to rouse himself. "If they get a toehold in Provincetown, it could be very bad," he said.

"Who?" Then I remembered. "The Lima organization?"

He nodded. "You don't want them here, Sydney."

"What is it with you and them?" I demanded. "You said you have a history. Is that all this is—a way of evening out some score?"

"In a way, perhaps," he said, and his voice sounded like it was coming from far away, some distant land, some distant time.

"Okay." I got up, smoothed my skirt. "I'm going home."

I left him there by the pool, staring unseeing into the water.

***

Ibsen was particularly strident when I got to the apartment. "I know, I know," I said placatingly. I opened a can of his favorite food before I even kicked off my shoes or poured myself some wine. I still had the Châteauneuf-du-Pape Guy had bought me, and there was no time, I reasoned, like the present.

My phone buzzed before I even had the cork out. "*Cara.*"

"Boy, am I glad to hear your voice," I said. The relief I felt was surprising, even to me.

"Lots going on," Ali agreed.

"You'll be here tomorrow, won't you?" I got the cork out and poured half a glass. All right, three-quarters of a glass. I didn't like the edge of tension I could hear in my own voice.

"Of course, *cara*. In the afternoon. Unless you need me to come before?"

Yes-yes-yes please. I mentally shook myself: that level of eagerness—or was it neediness?—would never do. "I'd love you to come right now," I said lightly, curling up on my couch, which promptly went into its Little Shop of Horrors routine and tried to ingest me. I wasn't even sure what I was afraid of, but that image of something dark and dangerous traveling at speed under the surface of things hadn't left me. Damn Guy for putting it there. I took another swallow of wine. *Get yourself together, Riley.* "You know Vincent's dead, right?" I could only assume he did; Ali moves in mysterious ways.

"Killed," Ali pronounced. "He might have drowned; he might have sustained blunt-force trauma to the back of his skull and died before he went into the water. Waiting on the report."

"You sound like a cop," I complained.

"I *am* a cop," he agreed. "But that's not why I called. I've been talking to Mirela."

Mirela! I felt a lurch of guilt. I hadn't followed up with her; too much going on. "What did she say?"

"She wants to meet with Guy," he said.

Hmm. I took a long swallow of wine while I thought about it. "Did you talk her into it?" I finally asked.

"*Cara*, to be candid, I tried to talk her *out* of it."

That wasn't what I'd expected to hear. "Really? Why?"

"Because she isn't ready. She needs to process this. She has Lily to think about, not just herself, and she knows it… but she obviously wants to get some clarity. I don't think she's going to just roll over and say all is forgiven…

I don't know what she wants to do. Which is typical Mirela, as you'll agree. And anyway, there's too much else going on there."

"Nothing Mirela's involved in," I objected.

"Guy's involved," he said, a little grimly. "Guy's involved, and you can bet she'll be, too, one way or another, if she does meet with him."

There was a pause. "Just how much about all this do you know?" I asked. "You seem remarkably well-informed for someone who's off-Cape."

He sighed. "I know Marie Almada's engaged an attorney," he said.

"That was quick," I said. I could have been referring either to Marie's action or to Ali's knowing about it. Or both. "This all happened *today*, Ali."

"I know." He wasn't going to tell me anything else. Probably just as well. "It's a law firm up here in Boston."

That meant something, but I was too tired to figure out what. "Is it a problem?"

"It could be. They have a decent track record."

"Track record of what?"

There was a long pause, and then Ali said it. "Breaking wills."

I took another swallow of wine, too fast, and choked for a moment. Ibsen finished his dinner and jumped up next to me. Ali waited. Finally I managed to say, "That means Vincent didn't leave her the fleet, and she knows it."

"Yep."

"And he left it to someone else, who might have killed him for it."

"Possible."

"But at the same time, it clears Marie, too, doesn't it? If she knew she wasn't getting the fleet, she'd have no reason to kidnap him or kill hm."

"You're assuming the motivations for both are the same," Ali said.

I felt too tired, too stupid. "You have to explain that."

"It's possible the murder was an accident," he said. "You said Glenn was getting the money, right?"

The shimmer of a ghost dancing in the corner of my eye, the giggle, and the echo of my father's voice, the pain and the astonishment. *I was getting the money…* I swallowed. "Yes. He had it."

"There you go. Even if the kidnapper *meant* to kill Vincent, there was no reason not to wait until the ransom was paid," said Ali.

I was still working it out. "But if she had him kidnapped so he'd change his will, then there was no need for a ransom at all." And if that's what had happened, then Vincent was going to be dead either way. You don't kidnap your husband and make him change his will in your favor and then show up to breakfast together the next morning as though nothing had happened.

I just wasn't seeing Marie as the mastermind here.

"There's too much they don't know yet," said Ali calmly.

"Who is the *they*, anyway? It sounds like everyone and their brother is somehow involved here," I complained.

Ali answered the question, not the underlying complaint. "The FBI," he said. "Police chief formally requested the help. But Julie has investigative privileges here too."

"Not the Staties?" In Massachusetts, most homicide investigations are handled by the state police, acting as the investigative arm of the district attorney, something that often rubbed local law enforcement the wrong way. Julie had had plenty of experience handing over her cases to the troopers. There are only four towns in the Commonwealth where local police conduct their own homicide investigation; Boston, where Ali's sister Karen was police commissioner, is one of them. Provincetown is not.

"The death is a consequence of the abduction," said Ali, blithely ignoring the fact he'd been the one to just separate them out. "It's a felony murder case. The felony is the abduction, and if an abduction results in murder, then anyone charged in the abduction is also charged with the murder. But, yeah, the state police investigative unit will join in, too. That's what I hear, anyway."

"Well, and add to all that, one Guy Husband," I said. "He's convinced it has something to do with the New Bedford crew wanting to take over the fleet."

"And then, of course, we can't forget to add Provincetown's own Miss Marple in the mix," said Ali.

That did it. "I am *not* Miss Marple," I snapped. "These are my *friends*."

We both were quiet for a moment after that outburst. I hadn't known Vincent. I didn't know Marie. But Glenn… Glenn was the one most affected, and I did love Glenn. I wondered what he'd do with the ransom he'd amassed. "I'm going to bed," I announced.

"I'll see you tomorrow, *cara*."

I clicked off, thinking we'd somehow just had an argument, but I wasn't really sure if we had, much less what it was about.

Morning brought no clarity on that score.

I poured coffee down my throat, fed Ibsen, and slipped into one of my reasonably-comfortable-for-hot-weather sleeveless dresses. This one was blue. I stood looking at myself in the mirror and decided it clashed with my green eyes and the shade of red I'd settled on for my hair (and what had possessed me to buy a blue dress in the first place?), and then decided I really didn't care. I pinned my hair up off my neck and called the toilette done.

My parents were in the breakfast room at the inn, my father reading the *Cape Cod Times*, my mother fiddling with her phone. "I was just about to call you!" she exclaimed when I came in.

"Good morning, Ma." I reached for the basket of Angus' pastries on the table and snagged a croissant.

My father looked at me over the paper. "Did you sleep well?"

"I did, thank you. And you?" But he was back to his reading.

My mother said, "I want you to take me to the dump."

I stared, convinced I hadn't heard her correctly. "Excuse me? The dump?"

From behind the paper, my father said, "She's got this bee in her bonnet."

"I do not have a bee in my bonnet. But you never told me about your swap shop, Sydney."

A waiter I didn't know intervened with an offer of coffee, which I accepted with alacrity. The swap shop at the transfer station is just that—leave anything you don't want, pick up anything you do. My parents live a life of—from my point of view—total ease in a New Hampshire community that on my snarky days I characterize as Stepfordesque. Free stuff is for people who can't afford to *buy* stuff, isn't it?

I took a quick swallow of black coffee and said, "It never occurred to me you'd be interested."

"Of course I am! We all have to stay inside a budget, Sydney."

Well, maybe. But our budgets lived on different planets.

From behind the paper, my father said, "Told you she had a bee in her bonnet."

"Edward!"

I drank more coffee. "Okay, sure, I'll take you to the dump. Not my idea of how to spend a vacation, but hey, you're welcome to it."

She narrowed her eyes. "Are you taking a tone with me, Sydney Riley?"

"Heaven forbid."

"You know I don't like it when you take a tone with me."

I glanced at my watch. "I need to go and talk to Glenn. Meet you in Reception in— twenty minutes?"

"Fine." She'd already gone back to looking at her phone.

Glenn was in his office, and looking, if anything, more unkempt than before. "You may be a bear," I said, "but you look like you're still in hibernation mode."

"What?"

I gestured to his head. "A comb wouldn't go amiss." I sat down in one of his guest chairs and softened my voice. "You okay, Glenn?"

"I don't know."

"Have you *slept?*" He sure as hell looked like he hadn't.

"What? Yeah, I slept. I think." He closed his laptop. His eyes flickered around the room before lighting on me. "Is this my fault, Sydney?"

"You mean Victor?" I was startled. "God, no, Glenn. You did everything right."

"I didn't call in the police," he said, an edge of desperation in his voice. "It was the police called me in."

"I know."

"I had the money." *I was getting the money…*

"I know," I said again.

"He saved my life. I should've been able to save his."

I bit my lip. "I don't think it works that way, Glenn."

"No," he agreed sadly. "No, I don't suppose it does."

He was well on his way to a decent depression, I thought. "You never talked with any of them, did you? Just got the messages through Julie?"

He nodded. "That's right. Maybe if I had…"

I held up my hand. "No. Don't go there. That isn't why I was asking, anyway." Julie had probably gone over the language, I thought, but it might still give clues to the kidnappers' identities. I was pretty sure there had to be more than one of them. Wherever they'd taken Vincent, he was a big man and in decent health. Conscious, he'd have been a handful; unconscious, one hell of a dead weight. "Glenn… Did you ever have any dealings with any of the New Bedford outfits?"

He stared at me as though I'd lost my mind. "The poachers? Why would I?"

I shrugged. "No reason." There was an al-most-audible thump in my mind as another theory bit the dust. I stood up. "I have to take my mother to the dump." I put a finger to my lips. "Don't ask. Are the FBI people still around?" They were the ones I really didn't want my parents running into.

Glenn seemed to catch hold of the thought. "Did your mother see them?"

"Not in any meaningful way," I said. "And I'd like to keep it that way. Ali's coming in this afternoon, hopefully he'll keep them dis-tracted."

Glenn grunted. "Only if you announce your engagement." He knows my mother.

That sounded better, anyway; a spark of a sense of humor is a lot better than none. "I'll check in with you at lunchtime," I said. "Oh, and before you ask, everything's on track for the wedding on Sunday."

"Nice to know you remember you work here," he said with a return to his usual grumpy self. I grinned and slipped out the door and headed up High Pole Hill to pick up the Little Green Car.

I was surprised to see both my parents waiting for me at Reception. I wouldn't have thought this particular jaunt was high up on my father's to-do list. "Dad?"

"Your mother insisted. She's looking for a lamp and wants me to tell her if it works."

There were so many things wrong with that sentence I couldn't begin to parse them. "Come on, the car's outside and I don't want to get a ticket."

The transfer station is on the other side of Route Six, backed up against acres of conservation land. I waved to the guys in the guard shack—all the transfer stations around here have guard shacks, God forbid someone should drop off rubbish or recycling without the proper stickers—and pulled up outside the swap shop. "There you go. Knock yourself out."

She looked at me, outraged. "But you have to come in!"

My father and I exchanged glances in the rearview mirror. "Of course, Ma," I said resignedly.

Inside, I left her searching for her lamp and greeted the volunteer watching over the shop—or, in this case, reading a newspaper. "Hey, Luther."

He peered at me over the *Independent*. Luther Beston, one of those guys—surely every community has one of them?—who has a PhD in astrophysics or molecular biology or something equally challenging, yet wears the same flannel shirt all the time, deals in junk, and has a front yard that appears to be filled with flea market castoffs. He survived on odd jobs around town. He was also, apparently, a poet of some standing in the community. Which just goes to show that, out here, you never know. "Sydney," he said, consideringly.

I sat on the stool next to him. "Luther, you know P'town better than anyone else," I said. "If you wanted to hide something, where would you do it?" I'd belatedly remembered my parents were in the next room and the word kidnapping couldn't be used.

"How big a thing?"

I swallowed. "Big. Like a person."

He didn't seem to find the question unusual. "Let's see," he said. "Lots of places. Over to the DPW, they have this whole big storage shed where they keep all the municipal lights for Christmas. No one ever goes there 'till November. Good place. Probably what I'd use."

I nodded. "Could be."

"Then there's the water tower," Luther said. "Water tower's a good bet."

"In the water?" I was startled. But why not? What if Vincent had drowned in fresh water? The coroner hadn't finished the autopsy yet. But it was possible... what if he had drowned in—ugh—the town's water supply?

"Don't know." He thought for a moment. "'Course, the best place of all is out to the old Air Force base," he said.

From behind me, my father's voice said, "What old air force base?"

Luther regarded him. "North Truro."

My father, now in my line of sight, pulled up a chair. "There's an air force base here?"

"Decommissioned," I said impatiently. This wasn't where I wanted the conversation going. "Ages ago."

"But it's still there? You can see it?" My father turned to Luther. "I was in the air force myself," he said.

Luther's face lit up. "Four Hundred Fifty-Fifth Air Expeditionary Wing, Bagram Air Base," he said. "Afghanistan."

My father said, "Second Air Division, Operation Tiger Hound, Saigon."

They beamed at each other.

Oh, God. It was Old Soldiers' Day at the dump.

10

And so we had to go to North Truro, of course.

The Air Force station used to be a thriving military facility. Or so I gathered; it was long before my time. I knew about it the way everyone knows about it, because I'd been out there hiking. It covers a tremendously big area, with all the barracks and outbuildings still standing, and a general Something-Untoward-Happened-Here feel to the whole place. In the barracks buildings there are the remnants of whatever they called their cafeterias, with the long serving tables seemingly ready to get warmed up again. There are the neighborhoods where married officers and enlisted personal and their families had lived, with forlorn crumbling bus stations and a playground with rusting swing sets and seesaws; you can peer into the small fifties windows and see what the houses were like inside. Some still have appliances in them. One has an ice tray on the counter. Even though the base closed quite properly and moving vans came for these people, it still gives you a creepy feeling everyone just suddenly disappeared one day.

It's all federal land, now part of the Cape Cod Seashore National Park, and there were decades of trying to figure out what to do with the place. The neighborhoods were completely abandoned; the houses all had lead or asbestos or something equally dire in them.

But over the past ten years people have tried to bring part of the place to life. It's the home of Payomet Performing Arts Center, where concerts and theatre take place all season under a tremendous tent. Various artsy-type endeavors are happening in some of the former administration buildings, too. They're calling it the Highlands Arts Center, officially, but everyone really just calls it the old air force base.

Luther was only too thrilled to give my father the tour. "It was built in 1950," he said happily. "One of the first of twenty-four stations of the permanent Air Defense Command radar network."

"What is *that* thing?" my mother wanted to know, pointing at the big balloon-like edifice over to the left.

"It's a radar station, Frances," my father said, a little impatiently. "What does it look like?"

"That one's still operational," Luther reported. "The FAA owns it now. So we won't go too close—they get a little edgy about trespassers."

"As well they should," said my father robustly. He was completely in his element. "Cold war, then?" he asked.

Luther nodded. "In response to the Russians testing their first atomic bomb," he said. "It was one of the first radar listening stations to monitor for Soviet bombers."

We were making our way slowly down the main street, heading toward the ocean; appropriately enough for a listening station, it was perched high on the cliffs over the Atlantic.

"I don't understand," said my mother. "Where did the planes land?"

"No planes," said Luther. "That's up-Cape to Otis, the air national guard. This was radar."

"No planes? I thought it was air force," said my mother to me.

"It was, Ma," I said. Maybe time to give the history lesson a miss. I didn't have either the energy or the knowledge to take that one on. "Come on, I'll show you where the people used to live." She'd probably appreciate the human element far more than the military one. As we walked away, Luther was saying, "In 1955 they built the Georges Shoal Tower Annex, which was located about a hundred miles offshore, one of the Texas Tower radar stations…"

We cut across through high grass (*ticks*, I thought in a moment of panic; they're a real scourge out here) to the neighborhoods, and even with the wildness creeping in, you can see what they used to be like, the symmetrical square blocks, very 1950s. Cul-de-sacs featured larger houses, which someone once told me had been for officers; rank does have its privileges.

My mother unerringly—she has some sixth sense—located one of the houses where the boards had been pulled off the door. "Let's go in!"

"Ma, it's not safe."

"Don't be silly. We won't be in there long enough to breathe anything toxic."

How long did she think it would take? But I followed her anyway. It's what I do. "Just don't touch anything," I said. I felt like I was the adult here.

"What a tiny bathroom! How did they ever manage?"

I peered over her shoulder. "It's bigger than mine, Ma." It was true; I didn't have room for a tub in my bathroom. The toilet was still in place, the mirrored medicine cabinet over the sink. It was only when you saw the places where the ceiling was falling in, the green slime growing up from the floor than it started feeling creepy.

"I've always said you should get a bigger apartment."

I let that one go. Year-round rentals in P'town are valuable as gold since Airbnb arrived and showed second homeowners precisely how much they could charge per night. I could barely afford my very small space but was enormously grateful for it at the same time, which said something, though I'm never sure quite what.

As my mother moved around the house and commented, I imagined the people living here. The fifties. A military family, which meant they'd only be stationed here a few years before moving on. Maybe she was progressive and wore slacks; probably she slept with curlers in her hair.

Of course, the bonus here was the view. You only had to walk a few hundred yards and you saw it, sweeping out majestically to the horizon, the Atlantic Ocean itself. Paradise. My friend Dana says we live in a postcard, and it's true. Even these people, transient, preoccupied, must have felt that.

Still, on stormy winter nights when the waves pounded the shoreline? Maybe not so much.

Nights out here make you realize you're in a rural area, no matter how many tourists make you feel otherwise the rest of the time, because of being in the middle of a national park with few if any lights. They'd have felt that, too, the isolation, the nights darker than dark. I seemed to remember there had been a rumor of some airmen having been taken up into a spaceship; the Cape has had more than its share of Sightings.

But the base was self-contained, so perhaps it didn't feel different from a thousand other postings. A bowling alley, a grocery store, a hairdresser, even a recording studio, it was all here. Up until 1994, when the Cold War was over and no one expected Soviet airplanes to come at the US through the Arctic, and everyone was sent to other postings, other towns, other countries, and North Truro was decommissioned.

And even the new breath being breathed in through the Highland Center's attempts at a miniature art colony wasn't enough to counterbalance the sense of sadness and decay in these houses.

We joined Luther and my father at the overlook, where metal sculptures moved gently in the breeze off the water and the sun sparkled on the waves. My mother, who had nominated herself the family's official whale-watcher, frowned at the horizon. "I don't see any whales," she said.

More to distract her than anything else, I pointed in another direction. "That tower you can just about see? That's the Jenny Lind Tower," I said.

"Wish I'd bought those binoculars," said my father, craning to see.

The tower emerged from the trees surrounding it like a castle from a fairytale, medieval as hell and strangely organic. "Jenny Lind was the pop star of her day," I said. "There's a legend says when she came to Boston her show sold out, so she climbed that tower to sing so everyone could hear her."

"It's probably not true," said Luther, ever a stickler for observable data.

"But it's a nice story," I said.

"What do you mean, when she came to Boston?" asked my mother. This is—what did you say the name of this town was?"

"North Truro," Luther and I said in unison, and he continued. "It was part of a railroad depot that got demolished. The owner had it brought here and reassembled over five years."

"Let's go see it," said my mother.

"You can't," I said. "There's no road going there, there's not even a path. It's just—there." I grinned. "An Outer Cape oddity."

"Plenty of those," said Luther, and my father grunted, probably in agreement.

"There's another legend," I said, and Luther rolled his eyes. "You're not going to go with that one, really, are you?" he asked.

"Of course I am," I said, and turned back to my parents, who were both still trying to make out the tower. "So you know why Guy was here that Christmas you came to visit, right?" Okay, so I hadn't meant to bring *him* into the conversation; he seemed to be in too many of those lately.

"Well, yes," said my mother. She turned to Luther. "Guy Husband She's talking about. It's his real name, isn't that amazing? We had dinner with him last night."

Don't remind me. "Anyway, the pirate who owned the ship he was looking for—"

"The *Whydah?*" asked Luther.

"Weren't you here then?" I asked. "I thought the whole town knew. It was another boat in the same fleet, called the *Mignonette.*"

"I was in California," said Luther obscurely.

"*Anyway,*" I said with some force, "the whole reason that pirate, Sam Bellamy, was there and not offshore where he should have been when the storm came up, was he was coming to see his girlfriend. Her name was Maria Hallett. She was supposedly watching when his ship went aground, and raced up and down the beach, screaming."

"Some people say," said Luther, "she had his child and thought he'd abandoned her, so she cursed him and that's why the storm came up in the first place."

"Whatever," I said impatiently. "The point is, she freaked out. And they say at night you can sometimes hear her screaming, and when she does, Jenny Lind comes and sings her sweet again."

My mother was staring at me. "You're making this up."

I shrugged. "Not me."

"Plenty more legends where those came from," said Luther cheerfully. "You ready to head out?"

But I wondered, as we made our way back to the car, how many of the young military families had heard that screaming in the night, and prayed to be reassigned.

***

I was late meeting the ferry.

There had been the prolonged visit to the air station. And then my father had expressed interest in checking out the golf club just down the road. Which left me and my mother staring at the Highland Lighthouse. "You want to go visit, don't you?" I asked. Of course she did.

We looked at the old postcards on display until my father and Luther joined us, and by then they seemed to have become best buddies. Lunch appeared to be on the agenda, and that meant, according to Luther, going to Blackfish in Truro.

Now, I'm no idiot. I can't afford Blackfish. Under normal circumstances, if anyone offered to take me to lunch at Blackfish, I'd be doing an imitation of a dog whose owner has just inquired if the good boy would like to go for a walk. But today, with the morning well gone and a sense of things happening in P'town without me there, I felt the slowness of the meal with every fiber of my body.

If anyone ordered dessert I was going to scream louder than the ghost of Maria Hallett ever could.

All of which meant ten minutes after the ferry pulled in I was running down the pier, sweat trickling down my back, madly dodging people pulling suitcases arriving for the weekend, and looking to see if I could spot Ali.

A line of people was trooping off one of the whale-watch boats, and I glimpsed Kai on the upper deck. He raised a hand in greeting; I flung him a smile, which was all I could really manage, and powered on.

And I seriously, *seriously* must consider working out.

Ali was standing talking with one of the harbormasters, and smiled when he saw me. "*Ecco, la bella signorina,*" he said, putting his arm around my shoulder and giving me a kiss. "Sorry I'm late," I blurted, and, belatedly, greeted the harbormaster. "Hey, Tim."

"Just catching Ali up on the news," said Tim. "Better go now, that car's been idling over there too long. See ya."

"What news?" I asked Ali.

"Nothing you don't already know, I'm sure," he said soothingly.

I gave him a fast, suspicious look. "That probably means the opposite."

He laughed, his voice liquid in the sunlight. "Come on, we'll compare notes. Where are your parents?"

"Back at the inn," I said gloomily.

Kai was ushering the last of the passengers off the boat as we passed, and I stopped.

"Hey, Kai, can I reserve a trip for tomorrow with you?"

"Not my department," he said cheerfully.

"What good are you?" I asked, laughing. "Kai, I don't think you know my boyfriend, Ali. Ali—Kai works at the Center for Coastal Studies. He's a naturalist on the whale watches. He might be able to get us on for free, right, Kai?"

He was laughing now too. "Still not my department, Sydney. But I can put in a good word for you."

"How many trips do you do every day?" asked Ali.

"Oh, no, you don't," I said. "You are not going to turn into a tourist with a torrent of questions. My mother is enough for me to handle. If you start doing it too, I'll probably jump overboard!"

"Wouldn't recommend it," said Kai, taking out a packet of cigarettes and lighting one. I stared at him, fascinated. I didn't think I knew anyone who smoked anymore. Well, Mirela, but she was getting more and more sporadic about it.

He inhaled and slipped the package back into his pocket, then started speaking on the exhale. "You have the shark-spotting app? Sharktivity?"

"No," I said. "I really don't want to know where they are."

"You've got to be the only one in town who doesn't," said Kai. And he was probably right. Shark-watching had become a hobby of sorts, with social media posts every summer showing close encounters and the scary dorsal fin protruding from the shallowest of waters, and it was another reason I swim in the inn's pool, thank you very much, and not in the ocean.

"I didn't see a single shark on the whale-watch the other day," I said. "Maybe they stay away from whales?"

"You think?" Kai was grinning. "Remind me not to hire you on as naturalist, Sydney."

"No worries. I'm *so* not after your job."

Kai said to Ali, "Sydney likes to pretend she's blasé about all things P'town, but I saw her on Wednesday, and when no-one's looking, she's just as excited as anyone on board."

"I was trying," I said with mock-affronted dignity, "to appease my mother."

"You just keep telling yourself that," said Kai. He ground out his cigarette and put the butt back in the package. "Well, that's all for me today. Nice to meet you, Ali."

"You, too."

"Bye, Kai," I said

"Good-looking guy," Ali said as we walked down the pier.

"Is he? I hadn't noticed."

"Uh-huh."

"Wait," I said. "Don't tell me you could be jealous, could you?"

"Not in the least. Besides, he's probably gay, right?"

I shook my head. "I don't think so," I said, trying to remember who Kai hung out with when he did winter trivia at the inn. "Not that I'd noticed."

"So you notice, do you?" He was teasing me and as usual, I was falling for it. "Oh, don't be silly. I only have eyes for you," I said. "And, besides, he's at least ten years younger than I am."

"A May-December romance," Ali suggested.

"Don't even think that. My mother will pick up on your vibes. She has specialized antennae for anything remotely matrimonial."

"I'm starting to get a clue where your career came from."

I laughed. "She considers it the ultimate irony. I organize weddings but can't seem to organize one for myself." Oh, damn. Had I really just said that?

Ali, fortunately, was unperturbed. "When you decide to get married, you'll elope," he predicted. "No way you'd want a busman's holiday."

"If I did, my mother would never speak to me again," I said. "Come to think of it, that's maybe not such a bad outcome…"

And then we were off the pier and heading to my apartment on Carver Street, and I was glad the day was hot, because my cheeks were flaming. Why on earth had I brought up getting married? It wasn't in the cards. The only real arguments Ali and I had were over our living arrangements—i.e., the fact that we lived apart. We'd reached an uneasy truce on that one–he wanted us to live together, I couldn't see the way to get there with our careers and homes and community attachments—and I certainly hadn't meant to up the ante still more.

One day I'll learn to keep my mouth shut, I promised myself silently. One day for sure.

11

I haven't ever locked the door to my apartment. It's not that kind of town. If I were pressed, I *might* be able to find the key, but I rather doubt it.

The problem with not locking your door is people can go inside when you're not there and wait for you. It wasn't an uncommon occurrence, and it was always irritating.

I'd been hoping for a few minutes of romance with Ali before we had to face parents and murders and runaway treasure hunters, but as soon as I opened the door I saw it wasn't to be. Mirela was sitting at the small table on the side of the room I euphemistically refer to as my kitchen, and apparently there was no getting away from any of it yet.

Ali's phone buzzed the moment we were in the door, and he frowned at it. "I have to take this," he said to the room in general, and walked back out the door to sit on the landing. With the door closed. Had to be work. I sighed.

"Mirela. What's up?" I knew what was up. I just didn't want to be the one to launch into it.

She had a glass of something cold and frothy and was rolling the base of the glass around in circles on the table. She kept her eyes on it, not on me. "Sunshine. I have decided. I want to see him."

"Okay." Well, I hadn't exactly *not* expected her to want to see him... but it would have made life a lot simpler. I glanced behind me; Ali was still on the phone. I pulled up the only other chair I own and sat down across from her. "Mirela, I need to tell you, I'm still a little suspicious of him. Of why he's here, I mean." *Okay, nice, Riley, articulate as ever.* "It just seems like he's really anxious to be part of this investigation. I mean, the whole thing with Vincent." Belatedly, I wondered if she even knew about Vincent. It seemed the whole drama was playing out at the inn, and I'd only seen her once in the past couple of days. Still, Mirela has her sources.

She finally looked at me. "You are saying, sunshine, one amateur detective who is anxious to be part of an investigation is looking askance at another amateur detective who is anxious to be part of the investigation?"

Well, when you put it that way… "Looking askance?"

"It is a fine expression."

"Sure," I said and shrugged. "I've just never heard anyone actually say it out loud."

"I cannot help what you have heard and what you have not heard."

Right. And anyway, I'd been the one to take Guy's case to her. I'd be much better at this whole thing if I wasn't constantly vacillating about whether she should succumb to his questionable charms. And looking askance at my best friend. I changed tack. "So why are you here? Do you want me to go with you?" *And please say no.*

She shook her head. "I do not need you to hold my hand," she said. "I am here at your house because it is where I told Guy I would be."

"Here?" I probably could have sounded a little more dismayed if I'd tried. Well, maybe.

"We are not meeting here, sunshine." Anxiety was making her even more abrupt than usual. "But I am not prepared for him to see Lily, and she is at my house, with her nanny. I am willing to speak to him. I am not willing for my daughter to speak to him."

"That's sensible," I agreed.

"Of course it is," she said calmly. "It is sensible, it is why I did it."

Well, this conversation was going nowhere fast, and Ali was still out in the landing on the phone. "When's he coming?"

Mirela's phone made some sort of sound, something like a baby elephant caught in a blender. She looked at it and said, "Now."

"He's not coming up here, is he?"

"No," she said. "You do not need to worry, sunshine. I am going now."

"Mirela," I said as she reached the door. "Be careful, okay?"

"Of course," she said. "If he is mean to me, I will kill him."

There was part of me that almost believed her. I'm not very good at telling when Mirela is joking. "Okay," I said, a little faintly, and she smiled, suddenly, and shut the door gently behind her.

Very gently.

Ali came in just as I was uncorking the wine. "Sorry about that."

"No problem." Neither of us holds a job that's nine-to-five, one and done; we each completely respect that work sometimes intrudes. It's one of the things I really love about our relationship. "You want something to drink?" Ali is Muslim—though about as practicing as I'm practicing being Catholic—and doesn't drink alcohol. Which can be both irritating and a lifesaver.

"I'm good. But should *you* be?"

"Be what?"

He gestured toward the bottle. "We're meeting your parents, aren't we?"

"Precisely," I said, and poured a glass. "I can't face my mother without some mood enhancer, especially not now."

He sat down and Ibsen immediately jumped onto his lap. Ibsen never jumps onto my lap. "Do they know yet?" he asked.

"About Vincent?" I shook my head. "Only that he's dead. My mother thinks I attract death."

Ali smiled. "Well…"

"Don't you start," I told him. "What do you know?"

He considered the question. "I know the earth is approximately four and a half billion years old," he said. "I know Charles de Gaulle was president of France for ten years. I know how to make tapioca pudding. I know—"

I cut him off. "You know what I mean," I said, and then, as an afterthought, "How on earth do you know about *de Gaulle*?"

"I know a lot of things, *cara*," Ali assured me. "It's why you're so crazy about me." I didn't say anything and he sighed. "All right, don't explode. Julie and I had a conversation."

He scratched Ibsen behind the ears and I could hear the purr from across the room. "The news from the coroner is, Vincent didn't have water in his lungs," he said. "It was blunt-force trauma killed him. Back of his skull was pretty messed up. He went into the water right away afterward, and that took care of the blood, washed most of it away. But initially there had to have been one hell of a lot of it—head wounds bleed profusely—so wherever it happened, there will be some traces, no matter how much cleaning went on after they got rid of his body."

"All we have to do is find the place, and it might point to the who?" I suggested. I knew all about trace evidence; I'm an avid consumer of detective fiction and CSI-type television shows. You can never get rid of blood, not completely.

"Or," said Ali, "find the who and it will lead to the place."

I frowned. "Not helpful." I took a swallow of wine and thought for a moment. "So, he *had* to have been on a boat," I said. "It's the obvious thing. The harbor's full of them. No one would notice anybody coming and going in a Zodiac or a dinghy, it's happening all the time. And there are always people partying, so even if he managed to yell, and even if someone heard him, no one would have thought twice about it."

"Don't put your theories in front of the evidence," said Ali. "It's an attractive theory, but that's all it is. And we can't have the harbormaster visit every single boat out there, not without a warrant. And we get *that*, there's nothing to stop whomever it is—still assuming your theory is correct—from slipping anchor and just leaving. In fact, if that scenario's right, they may have already left." He paused. "It's certainly what I would have done," he said.

"That's bleak," I told him.

He shrugged. "That's reality. But never mind, it's just one possibility. And even if it's what happened, they don't have to actually be in Provincetown Harbor to be apprehended."

"Apprehended," I repeated. "You're doing law-enforcement speak."

He laughed. "Easy to fall into. Don't worry so much, *cara*. Don't forget, the FBI is on the case. They have a lot of experience with this kind of thing."

"With head-bashings?"

"With kidnappings," he said calmly.

"They didn't seem particularly astute to me," I said. I was starting to feel seriously irritated. Irritated with Ali because he was right. Irritated with Mirela because... well, I didn't actually know why I was irritated with Mirela, just that I was. And above it all, what I really wanted to do next was sleuth, not go to dinner with my parents and struggle to hold my tongue so I didn't have to say the k-word.

It was there in my head, no matter how I might manage to hold it in. Not the k-word itself, but the actual kidnapping. I'd managed not to think of Alexandra for long stretches at a time, months even, or to think of her only in passing, the sister I'd once had, nothing that related to my present life and times.

But now she was back with a vengeance.

I'd thought she was the most beautiful person in the world. When I was little and my mother read me fairytales—hard to remember her in that role now, but she really had been kind of maternal, once upon a time—I always imagined the princesses to be just like my sister Alexandra. Alex was perfection, a perfection destined to remain forever unattainable because she had disappeared in the midst of it, before time and circumstances took the magic away. Like the princesses in the fairytales, like Sleeping Beauty, Alexandra was forever locked away at the perfect age, in the perfect moment. There was no time for anything to mar her perfection. Marriages, divorces, jobs, run-down apartments, financial difficulties, growing older... all the dismal parts of life never affected her, never had the chance to tarnish her crown. She never even had the chance to be truly human in my eyes. Only ever-beautiful, ever-perfect, ever-just out of reach.

If she were alive now, I realized with a bit of a shock, she'd be middle-aged. I couldn't imagine her middle-aged.

My parents' marriage had frozen, too. I've read most marriages don't survive the death of a child, with each spouse blaming the other for the loss, no matter how the child died. My parents had clung together grimly, going through the motions of Christmases and family vacations and graduations; but they'd stopped growing together when Alex died. Maybe they stopped growing altogether, not just as a couple, but also as individuals within that couple.

And maybe that was why my mother was so obsessed with marrying me off. To make up for losing Alex. Alexandra might have given her the white wedding she dreamt of. Alexandra was all promise and no reality. She could never disappoint. Her wedding would have been the most beautiful ever, her choice of husband the most amazing, her career the most sparkling. She would have been a company president or an astronaut or a bestselling author. She carried my parents' dreams into Never-Never Land, and I was the one who reminded them time hadn't stopped for me. Every mistake I'd made, every disappointment I'd caused, every failure I'd endured was just a reminder I hadn't been the Perfect One.

Based on the impaired decision-making that led to her abduction, I thought on the whole Alex probably would have messed up just as much as I eventually did, perhaps even more spectacularly. But that wasn't the image. That wasn't part of the shrine they'd built to her in their minds, and because it wasn't out in the open, it never got discussed, or contemplated, on any real level. I suspected at some point we probably should have done some family therapy around it all.

Well, *that* ship had certainly sailed.

I'd done therapy from time to time, in college, during my divorce, at various times since then, but even there I'd never talked about Alexandra. Never opened that door. Never revisited the little girl sitting on the stairs sobbing with the young FBI agent urging her to *breathe… just breathe… you're going to be all right, honey… just breathe…*

Ali said, "I'm not going to offer you a penny for your thoughts. Looks like those might have been worth a dollar or two, and I don't think I can afford it."

I came back to the present with a click that echoed in my head. "Sorry," I said. "Wool-gathering."

"From a particularly nasty sheep, looks like."

I grimaced. "Who do you think? My mother, of course."

"Ah. And, *cara*, far be it from me to be the bearer of bad news, but aren't we due to meet them... er, now?"

I looked at the clock. "Oh, damn. You're right. We're late. And I don't want them sitting around waiting, who knows what could happen."

"That's what I like about you, *cara*. Always looking on the bright side."

"Oh, that's me all right. Little Mary Sunshine. Come on, let's get this over with."

But I thought, as I closed the door behind us. I caught—just out of the corner of my eye—a shimmering in the room, the echo of a giggle. Alexandra was b ack and was asserting herself in a big way.

I had no idea what that meant.

***

We weren't just late; we were too late.

My parents were sitting in the lounge, both of them on the sofa, but at rigid opposite ends of it. My father stood up as soon as we walked in the door and shook Ali's hand; he'd always been slightly formal with any boyfriends I brought home, and even after several years hadn't gotten beyond that with Ali. My father isn't one for social niceties; he rarely talks much in social situations and Ali—who's pretty good at them— just baffles him.

My mother was holding herself rigidly in place and nodded when Ali said hello. God, I really, really didn't want to go here. This had to be at the top of my Conversations I'd Most Like To Avoid list.

Might as well get it out into the open. Pull the Band-aid off quickly. Whatever metaphor works. "What's wrong, Ma?"

She sniffed. "Excuse me?" Her voice was in the Arctic range.

Oh, God. We were going there. She was going to play *la belle dame sans merci* and I would end up saying I was sorry for something that wasn't my fault. She'd freeze me out and I'd feel desperate to get her back. We'd been doing this dance for a while. For years. For my entire lifetime, at least since Alexandra left.

But here's the thing I was starting to learn: we didn't need to keep doing it.

Ali squeezed my hand, gently, and I said, "Ma, you can either tell me, or not. We can either have dinner or not. But we're all tired, we've all had a long day, and I don't want to play games tonight."

My father was looking at me as if I'd lost my mind. Ali squeezed my hand again. My mother, if anything, managed to look even more affronted, and I was completely fed up. "Do you really want to talk about it?" I asked. "Okay, let's talk."

I drew a chair closer to the couch and sat on it, purposeful and more than a little scared. Behind me, Ali was still standing. "I'm thinking maybe someone told you Vincent Almada was kidnapped before he was killed," I said.

My father stirred slightly, uncomfortably. "We were sitting in the bar," he said. "The FBI agents were talking with someone in the kitchen, asking them questions, and the door was open. I don't think they knew we were there."

It was the longest speech I'd heard him give in a long time, and it indicated to what degree my mother was upset. I looked at her. "Ma," I said, feeling uncomfortable as hell and wishing I could be anywhere else on earth than with her, "I'm sorry you had to hear that."

"You could have told us," she said, her voice icy. "Do *not* pretend you weren't involved in this from the start. You didn't need to leave us to—overhear it."

"I was hoping," I said carefully, "that you wouldn't have to hear it at all."

Behind me, Ali stirred. "Sydney's been worried about you," he said. "She did her best to keep you from having to revisit difficult memories."

"Revisit difficult memories?" If anything, she was even colder with him. "And what would you know about it? You apparently don't know we think about her every day."

I sure as hell knew. No one spoke her name, but she was there anyway, the ghost of Christmas past, sitting beside the tree and making my mother bring out the sherry early, mocking me every time I came home from school with a bad grade. You don't have to say someone's name, you don't have to talk about them, for them to be ever-present.

Maybe we should have been talking about her all along. It was a little late to discover that. "Ma," I said, but then Ali had pulled out another chair and sat down next to me. "Mrs. Riley," he said, gently. "Mr. Riley. Sydney's told me about Alexandra." At least *he* wasn't afraid to use her name.

"I don't care to—" she began, but then—to my horror—he reached over and took her hands in his. "You know I work for Immigration and Customs Enforcement, right?" He didn't wait for an answer; he knew they knew.

"Law enforcement interagency cooperation is better now than it was thirty years ago," he said. "And so I've been liaising with the FBI."

I stared at him. What the *hell* was he talking about?

Ali hadn't let go of my mother's hands, and she hadn't pulled them back, either, both of which surprised me, but not as much as this whole conversation, which had taken a decidedly surreal turn. "I have some colleagues who agreed to re-open Alexandra's case," he said quietly. "Just for a second look."

"After all this time?" The ice maiden had melted and my mother looked as I imagine she'd looked that night in New Hampshire, raw and vulnerable. "Is there anything—is it possible..." Hope, now, the sharp painful edge of hope you don't yet dare believe in.

"I don't want to give you false assurances," Ali said. "And to be honest, I would have to say it's close to certain your daughter is dead. But perhaps we can find out how, maybe we can still give you a little justice after all these years. Or at least some peace in knowing what happened. I can't guarantee any results. But it's the best we can do, now."

I was staring at him. Nice to mention this to me before doing the whole victim support thing with my mother. *Wait until we're alone,* I promised him silently. We were going to have

Words, with a capital "w"... and then even as I thought it, I realized I was doing exactly what my mother had done, looking at myself as being at the center of the drama. This was Alex's story, not my mother's, and not mine.

Ali understood that. I was just a little slower to the starting gate.

There were tears in my mother's eyes. "Thank you, Ali," she said, and I looked at her in amazement. Nearly four years he and I had been together, and she'd never before voluntarily spoken his name.

My father cleared his throat. He must have been desperate to get out of there; he doesn't handle emotion of any kind very well, and this was verging on melodrama. "We have dinner reservations," he said. "At a place called..." He couldn't remember.

"Mistralino," I supplied. I didn't want to miss this dinner. Mirela swears by Ciro and Sal's for Italian food, but Mistralino gets my vote, any day. We were going to eat in the garden, with the fairy lights.

"Yes, of course." My mother withdrew her hands from Ali's, and stood up, all brisk efficiency. "And we should go."

And so we did.

12

Saturday dawned far too early.

When I say "dawned," that's—unfortunately—exactly what I mean. I'm not generally much of a morning person, and the last few days had taken their toll; I was ready to sleep through the weekend if I had the chance, but Ali was up feeding Ibsen before the sun, and making noise in the bargain. I found that thoroughly depressing.

I staggered from bed over to the stove and set the kettle to boil. "What is this in aid of?" I asked crossly. "You're well on your way to becoming *persona non grata* if this is going to be your normal morning routine." Not for the first time, I regretted having given up smoking.

"Ibsen was hungry," Ali said.

"Ibsen's always hungry," I pointed out. I spooned coffee into the French press, yawning, and sat down at the table. "That's a nice thing you're doing for my mother," I said. "Was any of it true?"

He looked startled. "Why would I lie?"

"I don't know," I said, shrugging. "I've always found it easier to let my mother believe what she wants to believe." I gestured airily. "The path of least resistance, and all that."

"I didn't tell you," he said, answering my real question and not the one I'd asked, "because I didn't know if anything would come of it. I didn't want anybody to get their hopes up. But since they'd heard about Vincent anyway…"

"So what's realistic here?" I asked. The kettle screeched and Ali went to the stove and poured boiling water into the coffee. "I mean, yeah, it's a great gesture and you may have solved a whole bunch of issues with my mother in one fell swoop, and don't think I don't appreciate it and all, but *really*? It's not just a cold case, it's frozen. I can't see anybody pushing it to the top of their to-do list just because you ask them to."

He put a cup of coffee in front of me. "Drink that, you'll feel so much better," he said encouragingly.

I grabbed his wrist. "I don't want to feel better. I want to know what's going on," I said.

He sighed and sat down on the bench across the table from me. "You know when you first told me about Alex I thought she might have been trafficked," he said.

"Yeah. And I also know when someone says elephant, all you can see are elephants. You *work* in trafficking."

He nodded. "I work in trafficking," he agreed. "And that's why I can see things other people might not." He caught my look. "Okay, listen. You sister wasn't abducted by someone who set out to kill her," he said. "It doesn't feel like one of those nightmare scenarios when the whole point is violence and assault." He was being delicate, but I knew what he meant. Serial killers. Torturers. Sadism.

"Thanks for that," I said. It had seemed pretty nightmarish to me, but there are degrees…

"And right away you got the ransom demand," Ali said. "That says there was a different focus—monetizing her. But—and this is where I think it's interesting—your family isn't a typical abduction target. You're not politically involved. You're not super-rich—oh, I know you've got money, but not the kind of money kidnappers usually go for. The penalties are huge, so no one does it for chump change."

"Like Vincent," I said, hearing an echo of Guy's voice saying the stakes were too low.

Ali nodded. "That points to a different goal, a different end-game," he said. "I don't know what the situation was with Vincent, that's a question still in play. But your sister... well, I'm still going with my gut reaction when you first told me about her. The money they wanted was never coming from your father. It was coming from Alex."

"Trafficked." I could barely say the word. I grabbed my coffee and took a sip. I was not going to cry. I was not going to cry. I swallowed, hard, a couple of times. "Then why the ransom?"

"Because it kept everyone in one place, worrying about getting money together in time. Waiting for the kidnappers to contact them. Focused. They probably took that one photo and had her out of Allston by nightfall." He paused. "Karen looked at the files." Convenient to have a sister who was also the city's police commissioner. "She said the police found the apartment two days later. Looked like several people had been held there. There were padlocks on a couple of the doors, and names scratched into the wall in one of the bedrooms."

I swallowed hard. "Was Alex—"

He nodded. "No one put this together at the time—I don't know why, can't say, not my investigation—but two other families got ransom demands at the same time. Same newspaper, same date, same pose. Not too much money, just enough that they had to scramble to get it. Sleight of hand."

I swallowed again. "And meantime…"

"Meantime, the girls were moved."

Breathe, Riley. Just breathe. Deep breaths. "You're saying she could still be alive," I said. "If she was trafficked, she could be somewhere now, she could be a—a—slave somewhere, right?" *Breathe.*

Ali shook his head. "It's doubtful, *cara*," he said. "But let's not worry about that right now. Not until we know more."

"I want to worry about it now!" This was worse, in a way, than my own nightmares about Alexandra had been. In them, she merely died, was killed, shot, strangled, something, a quick maybe even painless end. Now there was a realistic possibility she'd been taken somewhere and lived for years, maybe as a sex slave, forced to do unspeakable things…

"Stop," he said softly. "This is why we haven't talked about it yet, Sydney. You can't let your imagination take over. Let's get the facts first, whatever we can find out. Karen's got

189

some of her best people on it. They're talking to the feds. Let's let them do their job."

"When you say the feds—"

He nodded. "The FBI. And ICE. We're covering it all, *cara*." Nothing but sympathy and reassurance in his voice. I wished I could be anywhere else on earth. "So let it go for now. Right now, right here, you can be helpful. Try and find out why Vincent died. Help Julie and the FBI solve this one."

Well, that was new, Ali encouraging my amateur efforts. "You'll tell me when you hear anything? Promise?"

He stood up. "I promise."

I sniffed. "Okay, then."

But I wondered if, even then, he'd told me everything he knew. On balance, I rather thought not.

***

We got to the inn in time for me to do some of what was actually my job: there was a wedding scheduled for Sunday, and the wedding party had arrived. Ali went off somewhere, and Glenn hovered over my cubbyhole of an office until I started feeling claustrophobic. "Did the champagne arrive?" They'd asked for Perrier-Jouët Belle Epoque; we'd had to order it specially.

"It's been here since Monday," I said. "It's under control."

He snorted. "Yeah. Nothing is under control here. I'm never letting Mike go away again. Everything goes to hell when he's gone."

"See? Absence *does* make the heart grow fonder," I said. "Relax, Glenn. It's all good."

"You're kidding, right? I have law enforcement interrogating people on the premises. I have guests being inconvenienced. I have that horrible woman marching in and out of here like a major general."

"Which horrible woman is that?"

"Marie Almada. Turns out she wasn't too keen on Vincent giving up a kidney. And she has what-all to say to me about it. Loudly."

"Vincent isn't dead because he gave you a kidney," I pointed out.

"Huh. Tell it to that horrible woman."

I sighed. "Maybe it'll all be over soon," I said, as encouragingly as I could. Personally, I was starting to think it wasn't ever going to be over. My parents were scheduled to leave the next morning—five days together being about all I could take—but now with the news someone was looking into Alexandra's case, they might decide to stay on. That was all I needed. The afternoon wedding was for two men, and no matter what else was going on in her life, and no matter how I'd tried to get it across to her that gay is good, she would have something to say about it.

"From your lips to God's ears," said Glenn feelingly.

"Besides, it looks pretty quiet around here right now," I added.

When will I ever learn to keep my mouth shut? I jinxed us for sure, because as soon as I made the remark, Julie Agassi appeared, as if on cue, in front of Reception. Glenn groaned. "What fresh hell is this?"

I was just wondering how he came to be channeling Dorothy Parker when Julie came around the reception desk, making it even more crowded in my tiny fiefdom. "Did you know Vincent was married before?" she demanded. "Before Marie?"

"Hello, Julie. Nice to see you, too," I remarked.

"No," said Glenn. "Should I have?"

She glared at us both, then relented. "No, I suppose not. Sort of my job. I'm just feeling frustrated. She'll be here today."

"Who? The first wife?"

"Apparently she is in the will." She paused. "She's the one gets the fleet, not Marie."

I stared at her. "He left his business to the *first* wife? What, hadn't he bothered to update his will?" I couldn't imagine that one getting by Marie.

Julie read my mind. "Marie doesn't want it," she said. "She undoubtedly told him so, she's not shy about sharing her opinion. And as they don't have children, well…" She sighed. "There are too many people and not enough motives here for my comfort."

"Could this first wife have done it?" I asked. "What's her name, anyway?"

"Clara Benevides. If she did it, she did it long-distance. She lives in New Bedford."

Now *there* was a connection I hadn't seen coming. Julie zeroed in on my reaction right away. "Well? What?"

"Remember Guy Husband's theory?" I asked. "About the Codfather?"

"The *what?*" asked Glenn.

Julie shook her head. "We don't know if there's any connection between Clara and Lima's people," she said.

"So what? Twenty minutes ago you didn't even know Clara existed," I pointed out.

"Fair point," she agreed.

Glenn said, "I have no idea what you two are talking about. Just tell me one thing. This Clara woman, she's not coming here, is she? It's getting to be like a circus around here. I'm not crazy about the Race Point Inn being the center of operations for every cop in the county."

"You're exaggerating a bit," I told him.

"Not that much," he said grimly.

"Not right away," Julie said soothingly. "Well, she's coming here first, to check in, you do want to have guests check in, right? But she's off this morning doing something to do with the Dolphin Fleet."

"I'm going there this afternoon," I said, not entirely *à propos* of the same conversation. "My parents, Ali, God only knows who else. One final whale watch." Put that way, it sounded a little ominous, like the title of a mystery novel. One Final Whale Watch.

Julie wasn't interested. "I should talk to Guy Husband," she was saying. "See if he's followed up on his theory."

I pulled out my phone. "No time like the present." I also was itching to know what had transpired between him and Mirela. She'd tell me when she was good and ready; I wasn't prepared to wait that long. I pressed Guy's icon—which I still had, a year and a half on, don't ask me why—and was mildly surprised when he answered. "Good morning, Sydney."

"Um—good morning," I responded. "I wanted to ask you about..." I wasn't sure exactly what I was asking. Julie made a face at me and reached out her hand for the phone.

"About Mirela?" Guy asked. "She's fine. We're fine. But we're off-Cape, so—"

"Ask him about New Bedford," said Julie.

I was too busy worrying about what he and Mirela were doing together off-Cape. They'd only met up last night. If he was going to... His voice came through the phone. "Sydney? Are you there?"

"I'm here," I said. "Guy, did anything come of—you know, your theory about maybe the crew from New Bedford moving in on Vincent's whale-watch business? I mean, we—"

He cut me off. "That's where we are right now, as a matter of fact," he said.

"You're in *New Bedford?*"

Julie said, "damn it, give me that phone," and then when I didn't react fast enough she made an impatient noise, reached over, and took it from me. "Mr. Guy Husband?" she said, her voice pitched at the official law-enforcement-loud stilted level and tone. They must teach that at the police academy. "This is Detective Agassi."

Guy said something I couldn't hear. Julie responded. "Well, please be careful. I'm leaving a message with the local police. But don't do anything that—"

He obviously had no problem interrupting a cop. Maybe he'd picked it up in prison. Julie listened for a moment and then handed the phone back to me. "Guy?" I asked.

He'd already disconnected the call.

"Thanks," I said to her. "Mirela's with him."

"He shouldn't be there at all," said Julie.

"I'm more concerned about my friend than I am about your turf issues with the New Bedford police," I said.

Glenn said, "Would somebody please tell me what's going on?"

"Riley will," said Julie. "Things to do." She had to be irritated: it was the only time she called me by my last name. Good. She pushed her way back through Reception and was already punching numbers into her phone as she walked away.

"What?" said Glenn.

I sighed and summarized the situation. "Guy was in jail for a year in England and didn't tell Mirela. He's back to see if she'll forgive him so they can start back where they left off. Of course, now she has Lily, and that really complicates things, but I told her anyway because it's her decision to make and—"

He cut me off. "Never mind Mirela," he said. "What's the New Bedford thing?"

I sighed. "So there was this guy—not Guy Husband, another guy." Not for the first time it occurred to me what a ridiculous name he had. "He was like the gang leader for a lot of New Bedford fishermen. He cheated on reporting his catch and he laundered money and he was basically like the godfather on the docks. That's why he was called the Codfather."

"Bad pun," Glenn said.

"Yeah, well, I didn't make it up. He eventually was arrested and is in prison now, and he's excluded for life from ever fishing again. But he still has this organization out there, and since they can't fish, they're looking for other business ventures. They'll do the same thing with anything, they'll still cheat and launder money and all that, but they can't fish. They had to sell off all his fleet, and it was huge, I can't remember the numbers, but it was a lot."

"And Guy thinks they might have wanted the Dolphin Fleet," said Glenn, cutting through my babbling to the heart of the matter.

"Yeah, that's pretty much it. But you have to admit it's a big coincidence the person who's actually inheriting the fleet comes from there."

He shook his head. "If she's involved with this crew, then that's a good reason why they *wouldn't* have killed Vincent," he said reasonably. "They'd be getting the business through her already."

197

"Hmm." I hated it when a good theory went south. But he was right.

"All right," said Glenn. "Enough detecting for now. We still have an inn to run here, all appearances to the contrary notwithstanding." Notwithstanding? Everyone was using big words these days. "I want to know that wedding's coming off without a hitch, and if you're off enjoying yourself on a whale watch this afternoon, I want to know you have everything buttoned down tight."

"I'm not going to be enjoying myself," I muttered.

"What was that?"

"Nothing," I said loudly. "Glenn, the wedding's perfect. Twenty guests. Angus is doing the cake today. Florist is coming tomorrow to fill the bower. Adrienne the diva chef has a perfect private dinner planned. Dianne, the UU chaplain, has the ceremony all worked out. The Perrier-Jouët is all set. Nothing can go wrong." I was crossing my fingers as I said it, all the same. You never know.

"Adrienne the diva chef?"

I shrugged. "Come on, admit it, she is. I can't think of her any other way."

He shook his head, but a smile was beginning to twitch the corners of his mouth. "All right. I'll leave you to it," he said.

"Thanks a lot," I said. I really had no idea what "it" might be. Track down my parents. Track down my boyfriend. Try and get a look at this Clara woman and see if she looked the type to be involved with shifty waterfront characters. Not, of course, that I had any idea what type that would be. Maybe she'd carry a sign.

And, in all of that, *not* worry about Mirela off on the mainland with Guy. If they'd spend the hours it took to drive to New Bedford together, then they must have had plenty to talk about. Of course, this was Guy Husband we were talking about. He probably had a helicopter on call.

Ali was in the breakfast room sitting alone at a table whose detritus indicated the presence of other people, now disappeared, and was on the phone. He waved me over when he saw me hesitating in the doorway. "Yeah, okay, that's fine. See what you can do," he said, and disconnected. "*Cara!* I have good news."

"The only good news I want to hear is my parents left town," I said.

"Don't be like that. Next best thing, your parents don't need you this morning."

"What kind of miracle is this?"

He grinned. "There's a thing going on at the Great White Shark Conservancy at ten," he said. "I got them tickets. Pitched it as a marine day: sharks in the morning, whales in the afternoon. Your father wasn't enthused, at first, but your mother won him over. And she called me by my name. Twice."

"Must really love those tickets." I sat down and took his hand. "Okay, okay, I know that's not why. But it was nice of you to think of it in the middle of your other investigation and all."

"I'm not investigating," he said lightly. "Think of me as the hard-working spider in the middle of the web, sending out minions to do my bidding."

"I don't think spiders have minions."

"My kind of spider does."

I laughed and we ordered more coffee and it wasn't until later I remembered what spiders really do, and wonder what fly might be getting trapped in Ali's web.

13

We didn't have to wait long to meet Clara Benevides. It did really seem like the Race Point Inn was the hub of the universe as far as the investigation into Vincent's kidnapping and murder went.

It was Marie we heard first. Well, to be fair, it's probable that half of Provincetown heard Marie; it didn't take any great sleuthing on our part. She was in Reception and she was spitting mad. "You turned your back on this town years ago! How dare you show your face again?"

I slipped past Ali and made it to Reception before too many people finishing their breakfasts realized something untoward was going on. Thank goodness it was too early for the brunch crew; we generally had a harpist in for them, not Marie Almada screaming in a concoction of English and Portuguese. "Marie," I began.

Another woman was standing in front of the desk, her back to me. "*Vaca!* Watch out, Marie, you keep putting on weight like that, your little airplane won't be able to take off! What I do is none of your business."

"Vincent didn't want you back in town!"

"Oh! Is Vincent here to tell me that himself? No? I can't hear you, Marie, did you say no? Oh, is it maybe because he's *dead?*"

"*Ir com os porcos!*" Marie screamed.

"Same to you!"

I came up behind the woman and touched her shoulder and she rounded on me, ready to take on another fight, her fists already up. New Bedford style, I thought. This, then, was Clara. "I have to ask you both to be quiet," I said.

"Who the hell are you, sweetheart? This isn't any of your business!" She turned back to Marie.

"Um, it is, actually," I said, and she turned again. "What? You still here?"

Where was Mike when you needed him? Like Glenn, I resolved to never ever *ever* allow him to even *say* the word sabbatical again. "Ma'am," I began.

"Look who she's calling ma'am," said Marie.

I sensed Ali beside me. "I called Julie," he said quietly. "Maybe you should back off before you get hurt."

At that moment Glenn erupted from his office, and Glenn erupting is a sight to behold. I know him to be gentle, but he's an imposing figure, over six feet tall and while I've never guessed at his weight, it's well up in the high two hundreds. "Stop this now!" he roared, and even the two Portuguese women in front of him seemed to be taken aback. Everyone who was standing around staring took a step back. It was, in its way, magnificent.

I took full advantage of the moment. "Glenn, can we use your office?" It was the closest place with a door. I wasn't dragging them across the reception hall over to the lounge, even if they'd have followed me.

With the three of us—Glenn, Ali, and me—pressing them in that direction, they didn't have much choice. I closed the door gratefully behind us. Ali had come in and for a brief moment I flashed back to the last time he'd been in this room—and gotten shot. Not a happy memory. I pushed it aside and said to Clara, "Are you a guest at the inn?"

"Not yet," she said. "Didn't get a chance to check in before this *puta* attacked me!"

"Mrs. Almada," I said to Marie, and Clara snorted. I ignored her. "Maybe this conversation can be held somewhere else? Maybe Ms.—" I couldn't remember Clara's name.

"Benevides," she snarled.

"Maybe Ms. Benevides can check in and then you two can go wherever you need to go to have whatever conversation you need to have."

"I have nothing to say to this *puta*!"

"Then what are you still doing here?"

"This is my town, remember? You're the one took off! You left, and good riddance to bad rubbish! You're not welcome here anymore!"

Clara smiled, slowly, and it wasn't a particularly nice smile. "That's where you got it all wrong, *vaca*," she said. "The Dolphin Fleet is mine now and I'm here to stay. I'm back, and there's nothing you can do about it. So why don't you just get on your little airplane and fly away?"

Marie gasped. I think I might have, too. Glenn was still standing in the doorway, looking bemused. Ali said, cautiously, "It sounds like you have a lot to talk about, but this isn't the time or the place."

Everyone ignored him.

Clara wasn't one to not rub it in. "Vincent knew he could only trust me with the fleet," she said. "Not you. Not his *second* wife. Second wife and second-best, I always say. I was just biding my time. I knew I'd be back, and running one of the most lucrative businesses on the Cape, to boot! Maybe I'll take back the old name, too. Clara Almada. Has a nice ring to it, don't you think, eh, Marie?"

I think Marie was about to launch herself at Clara, but Glenn grabbed her first. It was a parody of the saloon fight scenes in westerns, him holding Marie back and Ali ready to grab Clara if necessary. And into this touching little tableau came Julie.

She wasn't taking any nonsense from anyone. Julie may not be Cape-born, she's a washashore like a lot of us, but she worked in a couple of cities I never ever want to visit, and she's as tough as any Portuguese woman, any day. "That's enough," she announced crisply.

Ali must have described the situation succinctly, because she'd brought two uniformed officers with her. They moved in smoothly and silently and each stood near one of the women. Glenn relaxed his hold on Marie.

Julie said to him, "Do you want us to escort these ladies off the premises?"

Glenn said, "I'm fine with Ms. Benevides checking in, as planned. I don't want any more disruption in the lobby."

Julie said, "Give us a minute."

Nobody moved. She looked at me. "That means you, Riley," she said. "And Special Agent Hakim. And you." She looked at Glenn.

"Come on," said Ali to me. "The detective has it under control." We trooped out of the office. Outside, interest was evaporating; it was, after all, a gorgeous Saturday morning in June, and the sun and waves beckoned.

"Whew," I said, and squinted at Glenn. "Did you have any idea..?"

He shook his head. "None," he said. "I don't even know how Marie knew she was here."

We stood about awkwardly for a few minutes and then the office door opened and Marie came out. She didn't look at us, didn't say a word, just marched out through the front door. I felt I could start breathing normally again.

Clara was next, with Julie and her uniforms behind. Julie, I thought, had minions. Ali had minions. I wanted minions. "Call us if you need anything else," she said to Glenn, but her eyes were on Clara. "Ms. Benevides would like to check in now, and she's going to stop by the police station after that."

"Not so fast," said Clara, but it was with just a shadow of the spunk she'd shown before. "I have plans for this morning. Meeting someone."

"Make sure you come by," said Julie, and the police contingent left.

Clara scowled in my direction before marching over to the reception desk and pulling out her credit card for the Handsome Young Thing who had finally managed to close his mouth. Glenn and Ali and I hovered, not sure whether it was safe to leave her alone. She sensed it, and turned to us. "You don't have to babysit me," she snapped. "I'm checking in and then I'll get out of your hair. And I won't pick any more fights out there, either."

Glenn said, "I don't mind what you do anywhere else. Just not at the Race Point."

Ali said, "But just something to think about, probably the best way to come home isn't to immediately antagonize people who live here."

I said, "Good."

"I'll do what I do," she said, tucking her receipt away in her shoulder-bag. "Anyway, I'm out on the water this morning, so unless Miss Cape Air Pilot there plans to swim, she won't be getting in my way."

I wasn't sure what else to say. Congratulations on owning the Dolphin Fleet? Were you involved in your former husband's demise? Do you know Marcos Lima? None of that felt any too appropriate, so I did what I almost never do and said nothing at all.

"I need some coffee," said Glenn and turned and walked into the dining room.

"And that," said Ali, "concludes our morning's entertainment from the Race Point Inn. Tune in next week when the battle of the wives heats up and…"

"Oh," I said irritably. "do shut up."

***

My next stop was to find out what was going on with Guy and Mirela. Up in New Bedford. Alone. Together.

I was starting to think Guy had more than one fish on the hook here, so to speak. He gets out of prison. His empire has apparently fared well in his absence—actually, I already knew that; divers from his exploration-salvage company had been bringing up artifacts from the *Mignonette* regularly since they'd found it; there was even talk of financing a traveling exhibit. But *something* had made him look into the New Bedford outfit (and was it only coincidence the Codfather was in prison at the same time as Guy, albeit an ocean apart? or was I leaning into some conspiracy theory here?), and it wasn't just the connection between Clara and Vincent, either. He'd brought up New Bedford before Clara was even on the scene. So what exactly was going on there?

And why did he have to drag Mirela into it? If these people were dangerous, isn't that the last place he'd want Mirela?

And on top of that... I still wasn't getting how you can leave the woman you supposedly love alone for almost two years without a word, a note, an email, anything. My friend Margo, who's an attorney up in Marstons Mills—and had in fact acted as Ali's attorney for a brief time during a fairly dramatic Carnival, once upon a time—anyway, Margo is constantly emailing prisoners in a variety of places. It wasn't unheard-of. It wasn't impossible. What had been going through his mind all that time? I sure as hell knew what had been going through Mirela's.

Ali had some telephoning to do and disappeared; who knows where he went. Maybe to my apartment. He and Ibsen have this thing.

I had to phone, too, and my little cubbyhole of an office didn't provide much privacy. I wandered out onto the terrace and the pool area; it was still a little early in the day for guests to start congregating there. Most were still nursing hangovers and plotting where to go for brunch; we're that kind of town in the summertime.

There was no one, not even a bartender, at the tiki bar, so I hopped up on one of the stools and pulled out my phone. What was

Mirela doing and, more importantly, why hadn't she told me about whatever it was? She'd gone from *absolutely not* to *maybe* to *oh, okay, I'll see him* to spending the night and traveling together, and all of it in a very short period of time, and I was suspicious. This wasn't like Mirela.

Mostly, though, I was feeling a little guilty; I had, after all, more or less argued Guy's case to her. Were we both going to regret that?

I took a deep breath and asked Siri to call Mirela, mobile, and waited anxiously as it went to voicemail. Damn. "Mirela, it's me. What the hell are you doing with Guy in New Bedford? Call me!"

I was still sitting there feeling baffled when Glenn strolled out. "A penny for your thoughts."

"Why's everyone offering me money just to think today?" I shook my head. "Glenn, what's happening? I feel like there's this huge—something—coming at us, a storm, something, and there's nothing we can do."

"Like the Nothing," Glenn said unexpectedly, hitching himself on the barstool next to mine. "You know, in that movie, *The Never-Ending Story*? The Nothing with a capital N."

"Wasn't that supposed to be an allegory about nuclear destruction?"

"Pretty much describes what you're feeling, though, doesn't it?"

I peered at him. "You feel it, too," I said.

He sighed, a big, gusty sound. "I feel something," he said at length. "What I don't like is that whatever's coming, it's coming here to the Race Point. The FBI are still here, looking official and scaring the guests. Detective Agassi's doing the same thing. The state police have been in. Marie Almada's in and out of the inn all day for reasons I completely don't understand, and now Clara Benevides is here, too—though not this morning, thank God, she checked in and then went out on the water."

"Probably inspecting her new business from close up," I said sourly. "I have to say, I didn't exactly take to her."

"But you took to *Marie*?"

"You make a good point," I conceded. Vincent had definitely had a type: they were both striking, dramatic, passionate—everything an innkeeper tries to keep out of his establishment. I sighed. "I don't suppose anyone's come up with a reason for kidnapping Vincent?"

"And then there's your parents," Glenn said, continuing with his own train of thought. "You know I want to make everything nice for them, but the guests are talking about the kidnapping, and I can't keep running interference."

"No need to," I said. "They already know."

"He stared at me. "You told them?"

"Not exactly. They overheard something—oh, and anyway, trying to keep it a secret, that was a stupid idea. My parents are intelligent and I was behaving like I was withholding information from a child, or something. I don't suppose saying Alexandra's name out loud made her any more real to them."

"And they're okay?"

I shrugged. "Maybe. Depends on what Ali comes up with." I caught his glance. "Right, I forgot, you weren't around for that episode. Ali's gotten the powers that be to reopen the case. My mother is now calling him by his first name and believing he walks on water. I'm not sure which extreme is worse." I sighed again. "And how bad it's going to be when he comes up with nothing. She thinks he's going to crack the case."

"He isn't?"

I shook my head. "How would he? How would anyone? It was thirty years ago." I paused. "He did find out she was trafficked," I said.

"That's what he thought from the start, isn't it? From when you first told him?"

"Yeah, only I was assuming, you know, you work in something, you make connections that might not be there. George Lakoff and *don't think of an elephant*, you know? But turns out he was right."

"I'm sorry." His voice was almost unbearably gentle.

I shrugged. "It is what it is." I waited, but there was no shimmer, no giggle, no ghost at the edge of my vision. Apparently Alex was taking the day off. "Anyway, it doesn't get us any further, does it? The two things have nothing in common. Just me, and I'm only accidentally connected to the Dolphin Fleet. Vincent wasn't going to be trafficked."

"I don't think they know what exactly happened to Vincent."

"And isn't there some statistic that says anything you don't solve in the first two days doesn't get solved?" I asked. "I'm pretty sure I read it somewhere."

He stroked his beard. "You're not the one expected to solve it, Sydney," he said.

"I know."

"You can't possibly blame yourself."

"I know."

"So don't do it."

"I won't," I said. We both knew I would.

"Okay," said Glenn. "So what do you want to do? Sitting here stewing isn't getting you anywhere. Your parents aren't around, as far as I can tell your boyfriend isn't around, Mirela isn't around—"

"You're making me sound like Little Orphan Annie," I complained.

He ignored me. "So you have a whole morning to yourself. I saw your reservations, you're going out on a whale watch at two-thirty. You could sit here and stew, or you could do something."

"Like what?"

"I'm supposed to know that? I'm not the detective here. Go interview somebody. Do something. Annoy the FBI. They still don't know where Vincent was being held, or not as far as I'm aware, maybe you can figure that out. Do something, Sydney, because you're looking depressed and we have an important wedding here tomorrow."

"A businessman to the last," I murmured.

"It's your livelihood, too," he reminded me.

I sighed. "I know, I know." I caught his look. "It'll be fine, Glenn. I promise. Nothing's going to go wrong."

"Okay. This isn't a good time to trip up. The *Cape Cod Times* has been lurking around asking questions of random guests, and once they get hold of either Marie or Clara it's all over. We'll have the *Boston Globe*, we'll have the national papers, who knows what."

He was exaggerating, but not as much as either of us would have liked. "I don't even know who to talk to," I said. "I don't know who knows anything."

"You know people who know P'town," he reminded me. "That's where this thing starts and ends, Sydney. It's not a national story. It's just us here. The Almadas have been part of this town for generations. The answer is in here, not out there."

"You really want them caught, don't you? Whoever did this?"

He didn't answer at once. A couple of guests wearing fluffy white robes drifted out of the spa and spread themselves out by the pool; the tiki bar was due to open and Bloody Mary's would be flowing. It was time to do something. Anything.

"Luther," I decided. "I'll talk to Luther again."

Glenn nodded and patted me on the shoulder. "That's the spirit."

I winced. "Don't use that word," I said.

***

Luther was, predictably, at the dump.

I'd reclaimed the Little Green Car from its expensive rental parking up on High Pole Hill (and yes, I do have a resident sticker, but you try parking in a town lot in the summer. You just try. It's worth the expense to have my own place). I'd reminded myself for only the fifth time so far this summer I needed to get the air conditioning fixed, and headed out to the transfer station, which in Provincetown is actually a pleasant place if you can ignore the fact that it is, well, a dump.

I checked in at the guard shack, parked the car, and eventually tracked Luther down, not in the swap shop, but examining some twisted pieces of metal that looked like a giant baby had been playing with its spaghetti dinner. "Hey, Luther."

He glanced over. "Sydney. Twice in two days."

"Just can't get enough of you."

"That's what they all say." He pulled on some work gloves and started picking at parts of the metal mess. "Your dad still around?"

"Somewhere," I said vaguely. "We're going on a whale watch this afternoon, and they leave in the morning."

"Interesting guy, your dad. You must have had some great conversations with him, growing up."

I've often used various adjectives to describe my father, but "interesting" had never figured among them. Luther was plumbing hitherto unknown depths.

I probably shouldn't have been surprised. Luther sees things other people don't. If he'd stayed in the professional world, he'd probably have a Nobel prize by now, have discovered a cure for cancer in plankton, or something…

I stopped. My brain had made a connection there, fizzing around like a demented firecracker. Plankton. That meant something; I just didn't know what. I'd been thinking about plankton, I'd heard about plankton… I struggled for a moment and then filed it for future reference.

Luther had managed to insert himself into the tangle of metal and wires. I hadn't responded to his comment about my father, and he apparently didn't expect me to. "Luther," I said, more to orient myself again than to get his attention, "you knew Vincent Amada, right?"

He shrugged. "Sure."

"I mean, way back when? Did you know he had a different wife?"

"Wasn't that long ago, Sydney," he said, still poking at the metal mess.

"How long ago?"

He straightened up, scratched his beard. "Okay, lemme see. I gotta say, probably twenty-eight, thirty years? Clara Benevides, right?"

"Right." Thirty years ago. It was, apparently, a magic number. There was a shimmer of light off to my left, a hint of perfume in the middle of the dump. *Oh, so now you're choosing to show up?* "Were you here then, Luther? Was it—did they get along, Vincent and Clara?"

"They got divorced," he said drily. "That's usually a signal things ain't exactly perfect, you know."

"I meant before the divorce," I said impatiently. The perfume was gone. Maybe I'd imagined it. "How long were they married, anyway?"

He pulled a big piece of metal from the tangle and it screeched, loudly, ear-splittingly. I backed off a few paces, and Luther threw his find out onto the ground near me. "Not so long," he acknowledged. He pulled a small flask from his back pocket, unscrewed the top, offered it to me. I shook my head and he took a gulp. "Okay. Seems I remember it was kind of arranged." He screwed the top back on his flask and put it back in the pocket. "She wasn't from here, for one thing."

"New Bedford?"

He nodded. "Yeah. Almadas, they was all fishermen then. Draggers. Not many of them in the fleet anymore, only the *Donna Marie* doing ground-fishing these days. Can't remember the boat's name, she ended up in Gloucester, that's another story. Family didn't pay much attention to whale-watching, kind of for wimps, you know? Whale watchers are all fair-weather sailors. Fishermen, they go out, no matter what."

I shivered despite the sun. In Lopes Square, at the foot of MacMillan pier, there's a small urban park with a very large anchor imbedded in the concrete. Tourists pose with it, on it, even. Hard to image the size ship that lost it; it's huge. It was found somewhere off Chatham by someone—a dragger, as it happened—from Provincetown's dwindling commercial fleet, thought to be off an old sailing schooner, and brought back to be a reminder, a symbol, that this town isn't just about sport fishing and whale watches and parasailing, that men here still go out no matter what the weather, no matter what the danger. "So how did a P'town fisherman end up in an arranged marriage with a girl from New Bedford?" I asked.

Luther shrugged. "Families, who knows? But young. Vincent wasn't twenty yet, Clara younger than him. The engagement, the

marriage, turned out whole time he was doin'
the payment-plan arrangement with the
Avellars to buy the Dolphin Fleet, and Clara's
there thinking it's always just going to be
about the fish."

"Wait. She decided to divorce him because
he was planning to buy the Dolphin Fleet?"

"No, no. Of course not. Just that people
change, and their spouses don't always change
with them."

I watched him for a moment, wondering
if he'd ever had a spouse, someone from back
in his MIT days when it looked like he'd end
up working for some high-flying international
outfit in Geneva or Brussels… "Did they have
children?" I asked instead.

"Nope. Guess old Vincent couldn't. Two
marriages without…"

"So she went back to New Bedford," I
said. Where Guy Husband and Mirela were
right now. That had to be a connection, but
what did it prove?

"Back to her family," Luther confirmed.

"So why doesn't anybody seem to know
about her?"

He squinted at me. "You're kidding, right?
You still talk about stuff that happened that far
back? Especially marriages… in with the new,
out with the old. I'll bet most people didn't

even remember he was married before... funny thing, though."

"What?"

He scratched his beard again, thinking. "I wasn't remembering it until now, but I heard last winter someone saw Clara at the Stop & Shop."

"Here? In P'town?"

Luther nodded. "For sure," he said. "I'm pretty sure I remember a few people talking about her showing up like that. Maybe it was in the fall, actually, now I'm thinking about it. Truth is, I don't really remember."

"I wonder why," I said. "Like that, out of the blue." It had to mean something; all these clues had to mean something. I just didn't know what.

Luther shrugged and went back to picking through the snarled metal. "Anyway, Marie wasn't around home then, or you can be sure the whole town woulda have known. She must have been assigned to a long-haul flight for a while."

"Well, okay, then there's that," I said. "Why does Marie hate Clara so much? I mean, she's the one ended up with Vincent, so it couldn't have been jealousy. Did they even know each other? Where's Marie from?"

"Somewhere up-Cape," Luther said. "Not a P'town girl, but a Cape Cod girl, sure. Cape

Air was just getting started back then, nothing worldwide like now, just the one route back and forth to Boston. No girl pilots, though. She came to town to talk Dan Wolff into hiring her and met Vincent at the Mayflower." The Mayflower was a restaurant on Commercial Street, a Portuguese comfort-food stop for decades. "Vincent chatted her up and she said she was a pilot and he said he didn't believe her. So she bet him an engagement ring she was, and then called up the guy living up at the Murchison estate back then who had a Moonie at the airport and she took Vincent up on an aerial joyride and he got her the diamond the next day."

"Holy shit," I said. "That's a hell of a story."

He shrugged. "A Cape Cod story, Sydney. Plenty of those."

"Sounds a little more like a tall tale."

"Marie's always been a little larger than life," he conceded. "And of course eventually she did go and get Cape Air to hire her—first female pilot they had."

It seemed to me Clara and Marie couldn't have been more different if they'd tried. Except for the loud part. "And she didn't want the Dolphin Fleet," I said, wonderingly.

"Never said she didn't want it. Just because she didn't get it."

I stared at Luther. "Did she? Want it?"

Another shrug. "Not any of my business."

And none of mine, probably, a fact I cheerfully ignored. I felt like I was tiptoeing around the edges of some truth here, I just needed to see it in the right light, to get some sort of handle on it. It was close. I'd thought Luther was the key, but maybe—sorry, Glenn—the answer was back at the Race Point Inn. Maybe Marie knew more about Vincent's death than she was saying.

Yet it couldn't have been her. She'd been in Saint Louis. She was doing long hauls. There was no way she'd have been able to be in two places at once.

But what about Clara? Was it possible she knew she was going to inherit the fleet, and wanted it sooner rather than later? Getting from Saint Louis to Provincetown would have been a feat; getting here from New Bedford was a piece of cake. Even with summer traffic, it was do-able in a few hours, easier still if you drove during the night.

I had to remember to ask Julie exactly when it was Vincent had first disappeared.

Of course, that was a lot to manage for one person. Vincent hadn't been a small guy—not in Glenn's category, but certainly too much weight for one woman to shift easily dead, or control easily alive. But maybe Clara wasn't just one person, acting alone. Maybe Guy Husband was right. Maybe she had taken up with one of Lima's lieutenants. Maybe…

Maybe I needed to start asking the right questions. Now all I had to do was figure out what they were.

14

I took the Little Green Car back to its parking place up by the Monument and walked home down the hill. I still had a few hours before we all, my whole happy family, had to assemble on MacMillan Pier for the whale watch. Ugh. I think standing in that line on the bustling wharf was maybe one of the best reasons for not going on a whale watch. Besides my utter terror, of course.

Ibsen greeted my arrival by making a magnificent deposit in the litter box. I swear he waits for me to come in to do it. Share the experience, all that. I turned on the window air conditioner, then duly scooped, holding my nose, and thought: waste. Human waste. If Vincent had been kept for anything more than a couple of hours, it had to be a place with some sort of facilities, if nothing else a place to dump a bucket.

Didn't that point to a boat?

I sighed. The reality is it was June, when quite literally anything could happen here. June is prime tourist season, and as Alice Brock once told me—she's the one Arlo Guthrie wrote *Alice's Restaurant* about—people come here to be wild, to act crazy, to do what they'd never do anywhere else. In June, you can see just about everything, from drunken drag queens sitting on the curb and crying over a lost heel, to young men with hard muscled bodies striding down the street in scant Speedos and lace bras, to lesbian couples with their families in tow determined to give their children a different definition of normal.

The point is, someone could march Vincent down Commercial Street with a weapon at his back and claim it was street theatre, and no one would turn a hair.

I fed Ibsen and scratched him under the chin and looked around for some evidence Ali had been there. Nothing particularly stood out, but I was kidding myself: I'm not the world's best housekeeper, and nothing short of a small pony would probably call attention to itself. I stood for a few minutes in front of the cold air coming from the air conditioner

and tried to marshal my thoughts. I was supposed to be *good* at this kind of thing, damn it.

I found Ali sitting outside at Spindler's
with an iced latte in front of him, reading.
"Why are you here?" I asked crossly, plopping
down on the café chair across from him. "We
have two outdoor patios at the inn, you
know."

"Wanted to get a book," he said, with a
gesture across the street at East End Books.
Jeff, the owner, was rearranging a window display and waved. I waved back.

I said, "Clara Benevides was in P'town last
fall."

"Nice time to be here," he said calmly and
sipped his coffee.

"Don't you think that's a clue?"

"Everything's a clue," he said. He sighed,
put a bookmark in to note this place—unlike
my books, which are wildly messy with
turned-down pages, highlighted passages, and
mad illegible scribbles in the margins, Ali's
books are always pristine and beautiful. I
worry sometimes about him maybe being a serial killer: a lot of them seem to attach that
same meaning and discipline to neatness and
order. "What do you think it means?"

"I don't know," I admitted, and ordered a latte when the waiter hovered. Might as well. "I was at the dump," I informed Ali.

"And you saw Luther," he said, nodding. Ali's never met Luther. Sometimes when I tell him some of the wilder stories, he doesn't believe Luther actually exists, I'm making him up just to pull Ali's leg.

"And I saw Luther," I confirmed. "He's the one told me about Vincent's marriages."

"Are you suspecting either of his wives of foul play?"

"Should I?" I waited while my latte was delivered. "I could really use some input here," I said. "This is your profession, after all, not mine."

"Not exactly the same, but I take your point, *cara.*"

"Cops all say they don't believe in coincidence," I said. "And, listen, Guy Husband thinks the Lima operation in New Bedford might be involved, and Clara Benevides is from New Bedford, so that bears looking at, doesn't it?" I actually think coincidences do exist, but far be it from me to contradict the professionals.

"How, exactly?"

"What?" I put my glass down. "Wait, why are you being like this? You're the one who usually gives *me* ideas!"

"*Cara*," said Ali, "figuring out how one person got killed in a small town with a limited pool of suspects and very personal agendas is one thing. And you're actually pretty good at it. But taking on a whole criminal enterprise with millions of dollars at stake is something else altogether. That takes a lot of planning, a lot of manpower, and, frankly, more official standing than either of us has in this matter. This is the kind of thing my agency is extremely good at. I don't think it's something you should be trying on your own, for a whole lot of reasons, not least of which is I'd rather like to keep you safe and sound—and in one piece."

I drank some iced coffee and glowered. I secretly liked the fact that he was protective of me. I also knew he was right, but I still absurdly resented being reminded of my amateur status. *I love you, but don't play in the big boys' league.* To be fair to Ali, that's not what he *said*, but that didn't change the resentment I felt. In my experience, emotions are rarely particularly receptive to facts.

Then I remembered something. "But Mirela and Guy are there! In New Bedford!

They could get hurt, too! Have you heard from her?"

Ali said, "Guy has some experience in this."

Great. The boys' club. I glowered some more.

He glanced over at me, drained his glass, and tapped the table decisively. "Never mind. There's plenty to be done here, and besides, we have your parents to entertain. They're leaving tomorrow, remember."

I hesitated. "Have you found out any more about…?"

"Alexandra? Not yet, *cara*. But I haven't forgotten her."

"No," I said sadly. "It seems no-one's forgotten her."

"And that's a good thing," he reminded me. "Come on, it's nearly lunchtime, and your folks will be back from—where did they go?"

"The Atlantic Great White Shark Conservancy," I said. "My mother's developing an obsession with sea creatures."

"Better than an obsession with your wedding plans, *cara*."

Well. Maybe.

***

Glenn was in Reception, pointing out a problem with double-booking to one of the Handsome Young Men. (I swear I should learn their names, but they come and go all throughout the season, and honestly a lot of them do look alike, to me, anyway.) He saw me and came away, shaking his head. "Where the hell is Mike?" he demanded. "This never happens when he's around."

"He'll be back," I said reassuringly. "And meanwhile, you're doing great, you know."

He glared at me. "There's no need to be quite so condescending," he said. "Speaking of which, your parents just got in."

"Wait, what? Has she been condescending to *you*?"

Behind me, Ali said, "I'd like to see her try."

Glenn shook his head. "Just noticing your interactions is all," he said. "Lunch is on the house, by the way. Since they're leaving to-morrow and all."

"That's kind of you. Thanks." I didn't know who could better afford the inn's food, Glenn or my parents, but it didn't matter. As long as I wasn't the one paying. Our tax returns didn't even speak the same language.

"No problem. They're in the restaurant already."

"No rest for the weary," I told Ali. "Let's go get this over with."

The inn's restaurant—as opposed to its dining room—was always elegant; it had that Michelin rating to uphold. White tablecloths, discreet servers, a harpist in the corner; we were still in full Saturday brunch mode.

My father half-rose and kissed me and shook Ali's hand when we got to their table. I leaned over as my mother offered me her cheek to kiss. "Well, how were the sharks?" I asked as we seated ourselves.

"There aren't actually any sharks there," my mother said. "Not *real* ones. I thought there might be a shark."

"There was a pretty big model of one," my father reminded her.

"Still, I thought there might be a real shark," my mother said. "Did you know Peter Benchley regretted having written *Jaws*?" she asked. "Imagine that. With all the money it brought in!"

"I didn't know that," said Ali, conversationally, placing his napkin on his lap. "Why?"

The waiter appeared and took my order for a Bloody Mary and Ali's for an orange juice. My father waited until he'd left and said, "Wanted to rewrite it from the shark's point of view."

"Edward, he asked *why*," my mother said, a hint of exasperation in her voice. She turned to Ali. "Apparently he and his wife learned all about the Great Whites, and they spent the rest of their lives—well, his, anyway, she's still alive—in conservation efforts. The Great Whites," my mother said, settling into her narrative, "have been greatly maligned."

My mother, shark expert.

"And such a nice guide," she went on. "She said she's a washashore, isn't that quaint? Apparently that's what they call them, people who weren't born here."

"Ma," I said, "I know. I'm from here now, remember?"

"Well, maybe Ali didn't know." There she went again, using his first name. It was a little disorienting. For years she hadn't referred to him in any way other than "that man." I welcomed the change, sure, but wasn't it just the tiniest bit *transactional*?

"I've heard it, Mrs. Riley."

"Oh, no!" she exclaimed. "Enough of that. You must call me Frances. And Sydney's father's name is Edward."

I stared at her in amazement. "Ma," I said, "are you actually deciding to be nice to Ali? Just because he re-opened Alex's case?"

"Don't you take a tone with me, Sydney Riley," she snapped.

"I'm not taking a tone, I'm just—"

Ali broke in, gracefully. "Thank you, Frances," he said seriously. "That means a lot to me."

Traitor.

The waiter reappeared with our drinks and set them on the table. "Did you have any questions about the specials?" he asked. "Or would you like to order?"

I grabbed the glass and took a good swallow; my mother invariably brings that out in me. Everyone ordered, and the waiter left. "You'll like the whale watch," my mother said to my father, miraculously changing the topic. "That young expert—what was his name, Sydney?"

"Kai," I said.

"Yes, Kai, that's right," she agreed, nodding vigorously. "So knowledgeable!"

I exchanged a glance with Ali, in which he clearly was signaling patience. "Yes," I said, as calmly as I could. "He does know what he's talking about. That's why he's the naturalist on board." I hoped he'd be scheduled for our trip; having my mother on his side to start with was a very good thing.

"I wonder if he's married." *Really?* It had to be a knee-jerk reaction with her. Seriously. She'd just gotten on board with Ali as a positive thing in my life, and she still had to look at everyone she met as a potential matrimonial option. Maybe she just couldn't help herself.

Also, as I'd already pointed out to Ali, my guess was Kai was at least ten years younger than me. Probably more.

I drank some Bloody Mary. I wondered if she'd be doing the same thing to Alexandra, if Alex had lived. And damn, after not thinking about her in any significant way for years, I was letting my sister rent an awful lot of room in my head this week.

My mother wasn't finished with the topic of Kai. "And is he what they call a washashore, too?" she inquired.

"I don't know, Ma. We're really not close friends or anything. Just know each other from around town." I paused. "I'm sure you can ask him if he's on our trip this afternoon."

Ali nudged me under the table. I nudged him back. What can I say? My mother brings out every childish instinct I have.

"We stopped at that Air Force base again on the way back," my father observed, clearly opting for an innocuous topic of conversation.

"What Air Force base?" Ali asked politely.

"Decommissioned base out in—where is it, Sydney?"

"North Truro," I said.

My father nodded. "That's it. We were passing anyway, on our way back from the shark exhibit."

"Great White Shark Conservancy Center," my mother corrected him.

Ali took a sip of orange juice. "Don't think I know about that."

She started to say, "But we were just talking about it—" I put my hand on her arm. "Ali's talking about the abandoned base, Ma," I said.

"Abandoned?" Ali raised his eyebrows. "Sounds intriguing."

"It's creepy," I told him.

"They did some good work there," my father said. "A definite asset during the Cold War."

"It's fascinating," my mother said. Once she latched on to the right conversation, it wasn't in her to let someone else do the talking. "All these old houses. It seems like something just swooped in and took everyone away. Like that place—what was it, Edward? In Virginia?"

"The lost colony," he said. "Roanoke. But this isn't like that. The base was closed, that's all. No one was kidnapped."

There was a short silence during which everyone, my father included, looked horrified at his choice of words. But I suppose it was on everyone's mind.

Ali cleared his throat. "Sounds interesting," he said, and turned to me. "We should go there sometime."

My father said quickly, "Well, if you don't want to go on the boat trip this afternoon, I wouldn't mind taking another look—"

"Oh, no, you don't," I said firmly. There was no way in hell I was doing another whale watch alone with my mother. "We're doing this trip together. As a family," I added, and watched my mother's reaction out of the corner of my eye.

She didn't rise to it. "All these darling little houses, you wonder how people could ever live in a place that small," she said.

They were all uniformly about four or five times bigger than my apartment. I managed not to point that out.

"And it was all so—oh, Edward, what was the name of that series we watched on the History Channel? Not that it had to do with history, I don't know what they were thinking, but it showed what things would look like and how everything would deteriorate if humans disappeared."

"*Life After People*," said my father.

"That's it," she agreed, nodding. "*Life After People*, Well, that's exactly what this place looked like. With trees sprouting out through the windows and breaking up the blacktop."

"Like I said, creepy," I told Ali.

"Another time," he said to my father, and I caught my mother looking at him in a way that can only be described as predatory. She was definitely revising her thinking about him. I didn't know whether to be pleased or frightened.

And then our food arrived and we didn't talk about the Air Force base anymore.

***

Kai was on MacMillan Pier when we arrived after lunch. "Oh, good," I said. "I was hoping you'd be our naturalist."

He seemed distracted, a normal state of affairs in The Season. "Oh, hi, Sydney. You're on the two-thirty?"

"Me, my boyfriend, my parents. My mother already pretty much thinks you're the cat's pajamas," I said. "We were on one of your trips the other day."

"Right." Of course he didn't remember. He did several of these a day, every day of the week, for four months straight.

"Well, it'll at least mean you'll get a good tip," I told him.

He was watching a group of people gathered around one of the harbormaster boats down on one of the floating piers. Behind us, a police car had pulled up, and the fire marshal's vehicle behind that. I followed his gaze. "I wonder what happened," I murmured.

"Don't know," Kai said, and then pulled his attention back to my face. "Sydney. Four of you? I'll hold you places up on the upper deck next to me. You'll hear everything better, and you can ask questions."

"That's great, Kai, thanks," I said.

When I rejoined my family, my mother was going on about whether my father's sweater was going to be heavy enough. "There's wind out there, Edward," she said warningly.

"I'll go inside if I'm cold," he said reasonably. Plus, inside was the galley where he could get a beer. My father was no fool.

"But you won't see the whales and sharks and birds from there!"

Ali's eyes were on the floating pier. A couple more individuals with "Harbormaster" emblazoned across their shirts had joined the knot of people by the boat. "I wonder what happened," I said again.

"Don't know," he said, his voice distant and distracted.

"I hope whoever it is, is all right," I said. Summer in New England doesn't guarantee water you can spend any time in without a wetsuit, and every summer at least two or three people with incipient hypothermia get pulled from the water and transported to Cape Cod Hospital. And that's without adding alcohol or pot into the equation, both of which usually played some role in any accident.

"They're letting people on," said my mother. "Come on, the line's moving, hurry, we want to get a good spot!"

"Kai's saving us a good spot," I pointed out.

"Well, we have *things*, too, you know."

My mother doesn't travel without "things." I wonder what trips to the park must have been like, when Alex and I were babies, how many bags she'd have for diapers, snacks, toys, wipes, first-aid, books, drinks… I couldn't imagine. I've not seen any pictures of her at that time, but I'd be willing to bet she had decent muscles. "What did you bring, Ma?"

"Well, you told me yourself you don't know what's in those hot dogs, so I asked the kitchen to make us a lunch."

"We just had lunch!" And, besides, eating hot dogs was one of the guilty pleasures of a whale watch, as far as I was concerned. It was certainly the only time I ate them.

She hadn't finished. "Some of those hand-warmer things, a flashlight, a Thermos of coffee, some Dramamine, two cameras…" Her voice trailed off as she tried to remember what she'd put in the two bags she and my father were carrying. We were better supplied than the Erebus and the Terror, I thought. Hopefully we wouldn't meet a similar fate.

Though they had a monkey, on that trip. I wondered if my mother had considered a monkey.

By the time we'd shuffled our way a few feet forward, a few more law-enforcement types had quietly descended on the pier. I could feel rather than see Ali watching them. "I'll be right back," he said.

"Oh, no, you don't!" I rounded on him. "You are *not* leaving me here alone."

"You're with your parents."

"That's what I mean!"

"I won't let it leave without me," he said. "I just need to see if I can help."

"All hands on deck," I said, and was surprised at how bitter my voice sounded.

The line moved again and we shuffled forward some more. My mother fished deep in her bag and pulled out sunscreen for me to apply to the back of her neck. "You should put some on, Sydney, too. I know how you redheads burn."

I stared at her. "Ma. Look at my hair. You really think this shade is *natural?*

"You mean you dye it?"

"Don't you remember what I looked like when I was a kid? Brown, mousy hair?"

"You know, I don't think I ever really paid attention," she said, musingly. "What color was Alexandra's hair?"

We were using the A-word now? "Light," I said. "Almost blonde."

"Did she dye hers, too?"

I swallowed. "I don't think so."

"It's funny, the things you can't remember," said my mother. "I remember some of her clothes, and how she'd just throw them in a pile on the floor, but I can't remember her hair."

I glanced at my father. He was staring straight ahead of him, determined to not hear

the conversation. "Ali will be right back," I
said.

"Will he? Good," she said vaguely.

We shuffled forward some more. Just as
the tanned teenager at the top of the gangway
was about to take our tickets, Ali came running up. "Sorry."

"Welcome aboard the Dolphin VI," she
said cheerily.

I herded my parents to the upper deck
where, true to his word, Kai had placed re-
served signs on four places. We could see up
into the cockpit, where a couple of people in
white pressed uniforms seemed to be milling
around, and Kai's own station with the microphone was right in front of us. "Well, this is
nice!" said my mother. "He's a nice young
man."

"He is," I agreed. I'd been trying to catch
Ali's eye since we'd boarded. "What's going
on?" I asked him, *sotto voce*.

We were standing, leaning on the railing,
our backs to my parents. "They pulled a body
out of the harbor," he said quietly, looking out
at the big shed at the end of the Cabral pier,
the one with the massive photographs of old
Portuguese women on it.

"Gosh. I'm sorry."

"It was a shark attack," he said soberly. He glanced at me, then looked away again. "She bled out. It was Clara Benevides."

I gasped, which drew a look from my mother, so I pretended to cough for a moment to reassure her. "Are you sure?"

"I'm sure that's what they told me."

"Are *they* sure?"

"Didn't seem to be in any doubt to me."

"This isn't a coincidence," I told him.

"No," Ali agreed. "This very much isn't a coincidence."

But I still didn't know what it meant.

15

Kai scrambled up and took his place as the engines churned the water around us. "Welcome to the Dolphin VI on this beautiful Saturday afternoon!" his voice boomed through the microphone. "In just a moment the captain's going to sound the horn, so you might want to cover your ears."

The horn duly honked. I could hardly pay attention; I was seething. Things were happening onshore, bodies brought up out of the water, clues sought, conclusions drawn, and I was stuck on a flipping *whale watch* for two hours.

"Do you think Marie killed her?" I whispered to Ali.

"I think a shark killed her," he whispered back.

Kai said, "My name is Kai Bennett, and I'm your naturalist on board this afternoon. I work here in Provincetown at the Center for Coastal Studies, where I'm part of the Humpback Whale Studies Program; I also help with the Marine Mammal Entanglement Response Team. What that means is I'm a scientist who sometimes gets to go out and do a little good on the water." There was a good-natured laugh from the audience, most of whom were more interested in watching as we maneuvered past the breakwater and out into the bay than in listening to Kai's credentials.

I whispered to Ali, "What do you think happened?"

He whispered back, "I have no idea."

"You're no help."

"Not my case."

"That wasn't what you said when you had to go check it out."

Kai said, "Let me see a show of hands: how many of you have never seen a whale before?" He waited; some people in his immediate vicinity duly raised their hands. "A special welcome to you," he said. "So I have a question for you. Where do the whales come from?" He took some answers, mostly from children. "Well, yes, now they live in the ocean, but do you know where the first whales came from? No, not from New York City." A smatter of laughter. "Well, scientists believe they were once land-based animals, not unlike dogs, living on the shores of the sea, feeding on—and obviously enjoying—seafood. They walked into the water, caught a fish and then went back to the beach to rest and sleep."

"He didn't say that when we went out before!" my mother exclaimed.

"Has to keep it lively, Ma."

"But over a long period of time," Kai continued, "maybe some forty-five million years, they stayed longer and longer in the water until they eventually didn't go back on land. The resemblance to these earlier dog-like creatures is still apparent, when you look at a seal, sea-lion or walrus. They can still lay on the beach or rocky shores. But what would happen to larger whales? They'd totally collapse on land!"

The kids had some suggestions around that, and they kept Kai occupied for a few minutes. We were approaching Long Point, its small squat lighthouse picturesquely Cape Cod. Today there wasn't a haul-out of seals on the beach, and people instead were sitting on the sand or paddling in the shallows; a couple of small boats were anchored nearby. I looked at the splashing and shivered a little. I was *not* going to look for dorsal fins in the water. I was *not*.

Kai's voice cut through my thoughts "Does anyone know what the biggest whale is?" he asked.

To my astonishment, my mother waved her hand. "The blue whale! The blue whale!"

Kai nodded. "This nice lady is right, it's the blue whale, which weighs about as much as a jumbo airliner! We won't be seeing one of those today, but what we *will* be seeing, I hope, is the humpback whale. That's our most popular summer visitor by far! The humpback whale is the fifth-largest of the big whales. Does anyone know why they're called humpbacks?" He was asking for trouble there, if there were any adolescent males on the trip. "No? Well, their name came from hunchback, which describes the way they bend their bodies just before they dive. But the humpback isn't just any old whale: it has the largest pectoral fins and is the most acrobatic. Humpbacks are very playful, they're very inquisitive, and as I hope you'll see, that means they really seem to enjoy the company of vessels and their passengers."

"That's right," my mother said to my father. "When we came out a couple of days ago? They really seemed quite interested in us, didn't they, Sydney?"

"They did," I confirmed.

Kai said, "And they sing a love song, which is the most complex of perhaps all animals. It appears all humpbacks within a certain group sing the same song at a certain time, then they all make the same changes to that song during the mating season and remember the song last sung in September, when they start singing again the following mating season in June."

"That's beautiful!" said a woman sitting near us.

"Pretty romantic stuff," Ali said to me with a smile, taking my hand.

"Please don't sing," I said to him.

"I don't know, I just might feel inspired."

Kai's voice continued, telling us what other fish, mammals, and birds we might be seeing on today's adventure. I tuned out the words and tipped my head back and closed my eyes. The sun felt warm, there was spindrift off the water, and everything should have been perfect. Except it wasn't. I didn't know how to fit Clara Benevides' death into the pattern I was already only guessing at around Vincent's kidnapping and killing. There was a connection, of course. Even for someone like me who went around protesting that coincidences do exist, this would be stretching things a little too far. Without opening my eyes, I said to Ali, "Someone really wants this business."

He was on the same wavelength. "They sure do," he said.

"Pity we don't know who she left it to."

"You can be sure someone's tracking that down right now as we speak."

I wished I could be there. Maybe I'd have some insight no one else would. At the very least, I could be a support for Glenn. Then again... I opened my eyes and looked over at my parents. I didn't want to be the one to tell my mother about Clara.

"Shark as murder weapon," I murmured to Ali. "It's original, you have to hand them that, anyway. And it has to limit the suspect pool a little, doesn't it?"

"It's been done before," he said.

"You're kidding!"

"Not in P'town," he added. "I've seen it in the literature. Australia, maybe?"

"Well, never say never."

"Apparently not."

We gave up on this cheerful repartee as my mother leaned over and passed Ali a bag of grapes. "Here, you should have something to eat," she said.

Kai spotted it, put down his microphone, and came over to join us. "Mind?"

"Of course not!" My mother gave him a warm smile and proffered the bag.

"Thanks." He helped himself. "What do you think so far?" he asked.

"My first time," said Ali. "Looking forward to seeing some whales. I've lived in Boston for years and always thought about going on one, maybe the one out of the New England Aquarium, just never got around to it."

Kai looked puzzled. "You don't live in Provincetown?"

"Just here a lot to spend time with Sydney."

"Who's never taken you out before," Kai said, looking at me, smiling and scolding.

"I don't go out to sea much," I said crossly and, thus reminded, dug out my Dramamine. "I can't help it. I don't like to think about there being miles and miles of water under us. Makes me feel like anything can happen down there." Like sharks attacking whale boat fleet owners.

"Not quite miles and miles," Kai said judiciously. "Remember that guy who came a couple of winters ago looking for that shipwreck?"

"Guy," I said, nodding.

"Yeah, some guy, don't remember his name. He found it in sixty feet of water. That's hardly miles and miles."

"His name is Guy," I said. "Guy Husband."

Kai stared at me. "You're kidding," he said.

I shook my head. "Cross my heart, hope to die."

Maybe not the afternoon's most auspicious wish, come to think of it. Ali was looking at me oddly.

"Anyway," Kai said, recovering, "depths are always changing around here." He popped a couple of grapes in his mouth. "That reminds me." He scrambled to his feet and grabbed the microphone again. "Folks, I was just reminded to tell you a little about the area here," he said. "Cape Cod is an extraordinary landform. Actually, it's one of the world's largest glacial peninsulas. The wide, sandy beaches are exposed to the North Atlantic along the Cape's entire northern and eastern shores. Blowing sands greet you most of the year, as do shifting dunes—each with clumps of clinging grass, engaged in a never-ending struggle for a foothold."

My mother said, "He's not talking about whales or sharks."

"No, Ma," I agreed. "He's a naturalist. He talks about nature."

She made a noise that sounded suspiciously like "hmpf" and ate a grape. "Well, I came to hear about whales and sharks," she said.

I exchanged a look with Ali. "Be good," he cautioned softly.

"I'm going for a walk," I announced, standing up and making my way to the stairway—though I gather that's not the correct nautical term for it—that took me down to the main deck. A beer might not help, but it would sure as hell not hurt, I decided. Standing in line at the galley, I glanced over to the starboard side of the boat and saw someone I recognized. Possibly the last person I expected to see on a whale watch.

Marie Almada.

An hour ago they'd brought the body of Vincent's first wife out of the water, and here was his second wife—and widow—on a tourist excursion *on* the water. And it made no sense at all.

I abandoned my place in line and slipped through the door onto the deck. She was alone, as far as I could tell, wearing not the pilot's uniform I'd first seen her in, but practical jeans with a WOMR sweatshirt over them. Hair pulled back off her face, eyes narrowed against the sun.

I took a deep breath and stepped up to the railing. "Marie, isn't it? I don't know if you remember meeting me at the Race Point Inn. I'm Sydney—"

"I know who you are." And none too pleased about it, either. "What do you want?"

"I wanted to say, again, how sorry I am for your loss. Your husband."

"All right."

Conversational impasse. When in doubt, just tell the truth. "I was surprised to see you on the boat," I said. "You didn't seem very interested in the Dolphin Fleet."

She half-turned to look at me. "I'm surprised you think it's any of your business," she said.

Miss Marple would probably have a quick repartee for that. I didn't. "It isn't any of my business," I agreed, nodding. "I'm just still hoping we can find out who killed your husband. That's all. Sometimes I—I help out that way. With the local police, I mean."

"Them!" A decided sniff. "I've heard that about you. A busybody."

That was certainly one way of looking at it. "Sometimes it helps to see a different perspective."

"Does it?" She looked away from me, back out at the water. "Come to think of it, it's a little surprising *you're* out here, too. You're a local."

"It's a family obligation," I said. "My parents are visiting."

"Family!" It came out as a snort.

We stood together at the railing and I wished I were back on terra firma. A fishing-boat was heading into port, the requisite cluster of gulls around it; as we passed I saw it was the *Donna Marie*, the dragger owned by Cape Tip Seafoods, its stabilizing booms still down. Tourists from our boat all waved madly; the crew kept working and ignored them. Without thinking, I said, "At least that's a Province-town boat, not one of the New Bedford ones."

Marie rounded on me. "And how is *that* your business?"

"It's everybody's business," I said reasonably. "We all want the fleet to survive."

Another snort. "What do you know about the fleet? What do you know about any of it? Christ, you have no idea what you're talking about."

I'd about had it. And I was starting to get a little scared. "Then tell me!" I snapped. "Tell me what I'm talking about! Okay, so I didn't grow up here. I didn't grow up part of a fishing family. But I'm here now, and I want to help."

"You think *you* can help? Can *you* change what everybody's facing? Can *you* go out, day after day after day, in the cold and the wind, and knowing one fine day you might not come back? All those boats tied up at the dock—do you think they all produce enough wages for their crews to live on? Do you understand what it means to be regulated out of your livelihood? You, sitting there in your pretty inn making Provincetown so special for all the tourists, what do *you* know about a hard life?" She shook her head and leaned into the railing, her eyes on the horizon. "You don't know anything."

I wasn't sure exactly what any of that had to do with Vincent, but I was the one who had changed the subject. Time to bring it back. Maybe a little less directly, though. "Do you come from a fishing family?" I asked. "Originally, I mean?"

For a moment I thought she wasn't going to answer, that she'd had enough of me, but then she nodded. "My grandfather. And then my father," she said. "My dad died out on Georges Bank. They gave up the search after four days. Coast Guard an' all. No one could survive very long out there."

"When?"

A shrug. "Years ago." And now her husband. "You'd think I'd want to stay off the water," she said. "And maybe I will. I'm here today for Vincent, Miss Busybody, if you really want to know. One last trip on his whale boat while it's still his, before that woman gets her claws into it."

That woman wasn't getting her claws into anything, not since a shark had gotten its jaws around her, but I didn't say that. "I'm sorry."

"Well. It is what it is." She sighed. "Sell my boat, probably. Maybe even move. Don't know if I can keep on living here now."

"Which boat is yours?"

She laughed, but there wasn't any humor in her voice. "Oh, I'm not commercial. I have a job, a career. I just have one of the bowriders over at the marina." She glanced my way. "A power boat," she clarified. "Just to go out in. Not far. Used to go out with Vincent sometimes. Catch some mackerel for supper, maybe. Or I'd go out when he was down the Governor Bradford with his buddies." She sighed. "Today's my day for last trips," she said. "Went out by myself this morning, whale boat this afternoon, then I'm done. Vincent's funeral is Monday. They put me on leave from Cape Air, maybe I'll go someplace for a while."

If Marie had a boat at the marina over on the Cabral pier, then she might know better than most what boats were coming and going, which one might have held her husband. And yeah, I was pretty sure the FBI had had several conversations to that effect with the harbor-master already, but this was here and now. "Do you run into the same people, over and over again?" I asked. "At the marina, I mean. Or in the harbor. I don't know much about boating, don't know how that works."

"You mean, are we all one big happy family?" she asked, with a sudden grin. "Hardly. Oh, they like it when the big yachts come in, the mooring or docking fees are great, but most of the townies ignore the tourists. And they're all tourists, no matter how they got here. What's that poem? By land or by sea?"

I wasn't going back to Paul Revere's ride: I had some more immediate history in mind. "When you were out today, did you see anyone you knew?" It was a long shot, but they do sometimes come in.

"What kind of question is that?"

I shrugged. "I heard there was some kind of accident," I said. I wasn't going to say everything I knew, but I could push the envelope a little.

Marie certainly didn't attach any importance to the remark. "Don't know anything about that," she said. "Saw a boat out from the Center for Coastal Studies, that's all. Doing whatever it is they do."

Short of asking outright if she'd seen Clara Benevides, I was stuck. "I'd better get back,"

I said. "I just wanted to say, again, how sorry I am about your husband. If there's anything I can do…" My voice trailed off. Marie had made it abundantly clear she didn't think there was anything I could do.

She looked at me, appraising. "I think you mean well," she said at last. I took it as it was meant—a compliment—and headed back up to the upper deck. I was sure my mother had plenty to say to me.

I was right.

***

It took me a while, but eventually I spotted the lie.

Thursday, at the inn, Marie coming in and screaming and upsetting everything. Julie calm and measured. Glenn worried. And me, as usual, asking questions.

I'd asked Marie if she owned a boat, and she'd said no.

I even remembered my reasoning at the time: people who make their living off the water don't usually take their recreation there, too: for them the sea is all too serious. Like an opponent one needs and hates and respects all at once.

I'd been wondering if Vincent could have been held on a boat. I still thought it was the most logical place, because—well, because Provincetown. But she'd denied it. What would she want with a boat?

Apparently what she wanted was to keep one tied up over at the marina on Cabral Pier.

It was a lie, and that should mean something—people don't generally lie just for the hell of it. But I couldn't see why. If I'd understood what she was talking about (and that was a major and perilous assumption), her boat didn't have a cabin. No place to hold a captive or to stow a body. So why lie about it?

Unless it was just a cultural thing. Outwitting the stupid police.

"Now that's interesting," my mother was saying, and I brought myself back to the present. "What? Sorry, I didn't hear you."

"You're not even paying attention!" she exclaimed. "Really, Sydney, if you didn't want to come, you shouldn't have."

"I wanted to come," I said. Okay, speaking of lying... "What did you say?"

"Well," she said, "no one said we'd be seeing a fin whale. I didn't even look it up before we came."

"You never know what you'll see," I said vaguely.

"I want to ask that young man about fin whales." My mother doesn't like to be caught out. She prefers being the one in the room with the most information at any given time.

Right on cue, a few feet away from us, Kai picked up the microphone again. He looked over at me and I could have sworn he winked. "It was great to see that one, even if just from a distance. So let's talk about fin whales," he said. "The fin whale is the second-largest species of whale. It is found throughout the world's oceans. It gets its name from an easy-to-spot fin on its back, near its tail."

"I saw that fin!" exclaimed my mother. Kai heard her and gave her a thumbs-up signal. I was going to have to give him a very large tip for putting up with her.

"Where's Ali?" I asked.

"Shush," said my mother. "I'm listening to this."

"Like all large whales, fin whales were hunted by commercial whalers," said Kai. "Whalers didn't actually target them at first, because of their speed and open-ocean habitat. But as whaling methods modernized with steam-powered ships and explosive harpoons, whalers over-hunted other species of whales they'd used for their oil, bone, and fat. They turned to fin whales, killing a huge number during the mid-1900s. Whaling isn't a major threat for this species anymore: today, the biggest threat comes from vessel strikes."

My mother turned to me. "What's a vessel strike?"

"A ship hitting the whale," I said. "Shipping lanes are crowded, ships go at high speeds, disaster ensues." I was scanning the lower deck for a glimpse of Marie. I was pretty sure she hadn't told me everything about why she was on board, and I wanted to keep an eye on her.

Ali sat down next to me. "*Cara.*"

I gave up looking for Marie. "Neat disappearing act," I said.

"You left me alone with your parents," he pointed out. "Anyway, I have not been idle. I have been on the phone. Mirela says they'll be back tonight, and we should go see Lily in the meantime so she remembers what her godparents look like."

"Pure Mirela," I said. "What about Guy? What happened in New Bedford? And why did she call you and not me?"

"I called her," he said, reasonably. "Guy says they're empire-building for sure, but not in P'town. Apparently the tourist trade doesn't jell with their bad-boy reputation."

"He said that?"

"No; I interpret, *cara*. They're going after *him*, in fact. He's been on the phone all morning to his lawyers. It's complicated—not all Guy's crew stayed on the straight and narrow while he was off in prison, and a lot of goings-on in New Bedford he needs to sort out. He was going to check it out after he came to P'town to see Mirela, but he got a little side-tracked with Vincent, and made the connection because it was top-of-mind for him. He's pretty confident it's going to work out. But they're not behind all this."

"And what about Mirela?"

"Mirela doesn't know about Mirela," he said judiciously. "You know her. Always in control, always on top of things. He was heading off to New Bedford to check things out anyway, and she made him take her with him."

"You mean the little trip together was *Mirela's* idea?"

He nodded. "You ever see Mirela do anything that was anybody else's idea? She says it was so he could prove something to her."

"Meaning…?"

"Meaning something between her and Guy she's not sharing with me."

"That's disappointing," I said on a sigh, then caught his expression. "No, no, I didn't mean her and Guy. Whatever. I mean it's disappointing the gang up in New Bedford isn't involved with Vincent and Clara's murders. We have a rapidly shrinking suspect pool. As in, nobody." Maybe. I still wondered why Marie was on the trip this afternoon.

"You don't know Clara was murdered," Ali said. "I had a word with Julie about that, too."

"You'll do anything not to talk to my mother."

"So true. Some tourists found Clara; she was right in the shallows at Long Point."

I stared at him. *Long Point?* Before the Great Whites changed their address to Cape Cod zip codes, the Swim for Life route had stretched across the harbor, from Long Point to the Boatslip on Commercial Street. The point being, Long Point wasn't that far away. Only the most determined and hardiest of souls walked out from the breakwater in the west end of town—you can do it, it's just a long, hot slog. Pretty much everyone goes by boat, either their own or the pontoon water-taxi from Flyer's. And on a day in June? I won't say it's crowded out there, but it's sure as hell not solitary, either. "Did anyone see it happen?" I asked. "The shark attack?" If it had happened in the shallows, someone must have seen it. I couldn't imagine it was something you could confuse with anything else.

"Nothing. Julie said they all cleared out fast once they saw the body. She's been track-ing them down."

"So it might not have happened at Long Point." That made more sense; I couldn't imagine Clara had taken this opportunity to spend a morning on the beach. Then I remembered. "Ali! Marie Almada was out on her boat this morning! And she lied about having one, too. She told the police she doesn't have a boat." Well, technically she'd told *me* that, but Julie had been in the room. "She could have taken Clara out for a ride to be alone and patch things up between them."

Ali was skeptical. "Would you go out alone with Marie if you were Clara?"

No; of course not. It was as absurd as positing murder by shark. But that's still what had happened: that attack was no accident. "Marie's here," I said. "As in, on the whale-watch boat here, with us. She says it's one last trip, a kind of tribute to Vincent."

"Do you believe her?"

I shook my head. "I have no idea what to believe," I said.

"Hmm." He thought for a moment. "I asked who gets the business, now," he said suddenly. "It's layers and layers of lawyers, of course, but Julie said there's a son somewhere."

"Clara Benevides had a son? With whom?"

Ali shrugged. "Like I said, it's all tied up in legalese. Who knows where he is. It's something that'll keep people occupied for months."

"And what about the Dolphin Fleet in the meantime?" I asked. "They won't close it down, right?"

"Are you kidding? Something this lucrative? Not in a million years."

"That's something, anyway." I put my head on his shoulder and sighed. Kai's voice was talking about shorebirds, a not-unpleasant droning in the background. The sun was hot, the air tinged with salt spray, and Ali's fingers were laced in mine. I had to remember how lucky I was. How practically perfect my life. "This isn't such a bad thing, after all," I murmured to Ali.

"What isn't?"

"Going on a whale watch."

He chuckled. "Not bad at all, *cara*," he said. "Not bad at all."

16

Glenn had sent a car for my parents, which was beyond thoughtful. They were both looking a little tired, and for the first time in my life I was thinking about their mortality. I hadn't really considered it before. They were just always going to be there, annoying but stable.

I sure as hell wasn't going to think about it now.

Marie was already on the pier while we were still standing in line, waiting to disembark. "We should see where she goes," I said. I was pretty sure Marie was a major clue, if not the murderer herself. Like I said, our suspect pool was rapidly shrinking. I turned to Ali. "Would you mind? I need to get my parents back to the inn."

"You sure?"

I nodded. "Go!" I watched as he delicately threaded his way through the throng. A smile here, a murmured excuse there; people instinctively did what Ali wanted them to. Then I lost sight of him as my mother started talking about dinner. We do have that in common, she and I: we love our food.

We were nearly last off the boat, mostly because at the last minute my father had to go use the restroom, which got me thinking again about their mortality. I was more than relieved to see one of the inn's cars waiting, and one of Glenn's Handsome Young Men leaning against it. "Hey, Sydney, I'll drive you guys back."

"Thanks, um," I said, wondering what his name was. I turned to my parents. "Here you go. Why don't you go back to your room for a while and rest? I'm going to track Ali down and we'll join you later. We have seven o'clock reservations, so you have a couple of hours to just hang out."

"At the restaurant?" my father said hopefully.

"Of course," I said. I'd spent ten minutes wrangling with Martin over Saturday-night-in-June reservations. "It's your last night here, we have to live it up! I'll see you soon." They tucked themselves into the back of the car and it pulled away.

The pier was still busy; it always is, in the summer. Another Boston ferry would be pulling in soon; there was already a line of visitors with their rolling suitcases, victims of Saturday turnovers in town, regretfully going home. Across the way some kids were jumping into the water. I couldn't see either Ali or Marie.

"Sydney!" I jumped a little, then saw it was only Kai. "Oops. Sorry to scare you," he said. "Want a ride?" Behind him the deckhands were moving through the boat, readying it for its next trip out. "I'm done for the day, and Carol left me the Center's car." He gestured toward a Toyota sitting nearby and clearly earning the wrath of one of the harbormasters, whose job was to keep the pier clear. "Unless you really want to walk through that crowd."

I gave up. Ali was a big boy; he could handle following Marie by himself, and no doubt would be back at the inn in time for dinner—my father isn't the only one who goes a little nutty over Adrienne the diva chef. "Sure," I said to Kai. "I'd really appreciate it." Town was hot and crowded and the thought of an air-conditioned car was heavenly.

"Great. Come on, let's go before Dan decides to give me a ticket."

I laughed. "More likely push the car off the pier," I said. "He has a murderous look about him."

The things one says.

Kai popped the passenger door open and I got in, waving at the harbormaster. Kai expertly turned the car around, managing to hit none of the tourists milling apparently aimlessly about, which was a feat in itself, and we headed down the pier. I was still scanning faces around me, looking for Ali or Marie. "Your mother," said Kai. "How often does she come visit?"

I gave him a look. "Not as often as she wants to, much more often than I want her to, which is actually pretty much never."

He laughed. "Families," he said.

I looked at him. "What about you? Tell me you have mother issues, okay? Even if it's not true. Humor me. I don't want to feel I'm the only one with a crazy mother."

"Oh," said Kai. "Sorry, can't help there. My mother's dead."

"I'm sorry."

He shrugged. "It happens." We'd negotiated Standish Street and were on Bradford; it's the only way to access the east end, as Commercial Street runs one way only. At one point you take one of the side-streets beyond the inn to double back on it.

We'd just missed the street.

"You know where the Race Point is, right?" I asked Kai. "You can take the next one."

Kai didn't say anything, but there was a decisive click by my right shoulder as he engaged the lock on my door.

This wasn't good. Of course I said the most ridiculous thing possible. "What are you doing?"

"I thought we could go for a ride," said Kai. "Get out of town. I heard you took your parents out to the old air force base."

"Yes," I said warily. "So what?"

He shrugged. "Nice place to have a quiet talk."

"I don't think I want a quiet talk," I said. I moved my hand as slowly as I could toward my pocket. Where my phone was.

"Sydney, you know, this doesn't have to be unpleasant," said Kai. "I like you a lot. Always have. You're a nice woman. There's no reason for this to be a problem. But if you keep reaching for your phone, it will be."

Breathe, Riley. Just breathe. You're okay. Just breathe. "Okay," I said. "Just tell me why you killed Vincent," I said.

He glanced at me, then quickly back at the road. We were on Route Six, with Pilgrim Lake coming up on our left and the dunes beyond it. "What makes you think I killed Vincent?"

I shrugged. "So if you didn't, why are we taking this drive?"

"Fair point," he conceded. "You know, I think before we talk anymore, I'd like you to give me your phone. These gadgets are so smart these days, you never know what could get voice-activated. Do it slowly. I'd hate to have us go off the road because you did something silly."

I pulled the phone out and for one moment considered yelling for Siri to call Ali, but Kai and I were sitting too close together for that to work. I handed it over.

"Thank you." He tucked the phone into the side-pocket on his door.

I said, "So what's the plan here? You know my boyfriend's in law enforcement. You know if anything happens to me—"

"—he'll make it his life's endeavor to come after me and bring me to justice, yadda, yadda," said Kai. "Let's just assume you gave me the lecture and I heard it, okay? Anyway, I'm hoping we can resolve all this without resorting to any kind of violence. I don't want to hurt you. That's not my intention."

"So again I ask," I said, "what's the plan here?" We'd passed Day's Cottages and were taking the turnoff for North Truro. He really *was* taking me out to the air force base. I couldn't imagine why. There would be people there; chances were good there was a performance tonight at the Payomet Performing Art Center's tent. Throwing me off the cliff seemed a little dramatic.

I glanced at him, the handsome profile, the sheer youth of him. Kai Bennett. A nice guy. Even, in fact, even if anything a little *dull*.

He wasn't being dull right now.

"It's you, isn't it?" I asked. "Otherwise there wouldn't be any reason for us to have a little talk up at the air force base. You think I was about to figure out it was you."

"Were you?"

I swallowed. "No."

He laughed. "See, that's where you're wrong, Sydney. Your reputation precedes you. You'd get it sooner or later, and I can't risk it being sooner. I'm not staying around. I got what I came for. I'm hitting the road, but I don't need anybody coming after me."

"What do you mean, what you came for?" I demanded. "Kai, you've been with the Center for *years!*"

"Four," he agreed, nodding. "I had to wait until the time was right. In the meantime, I like my job. I never really wanted to do anything else." His voice was steady, reasonable.

I was still trying to wrap my head around Kai as villain. "I'm feeling really stupid here," I said. "Help me out. Did you actually come to P'town four years ago just to kidnap Vincent?"

He nodded and negotiated the turn onto Old Dewline Road. "It all went wrong, though," he said, and again the voice sounded utterly reasonable. Until you focused on what it was saying. "It was such a simple plan, and I still can't believe how wrong it went." He pulled into the parking area for Payomet and cut the ignition. There was a long pause. "You're probably thinking I'm crazy about now, don't you?"

"The thought had occurred," I admitted.

"Vincent Almada was my father," Kai said. "Did you know that? Of course you didn't. He never bothered with me. Just went on with his life. No money, even though we struggled. I had to get a scholarship for college, worked my ass off, grants for grad school. He never cared. I kept thinking, he'll show up for something. He'll show up for my birthday. He'll show up for graduation. He'll say he's proud of me. He gets this whole fleet of whale boats and didn't even recognize me when I came to work on one." He swallowed. "He didn't care. I just wanted him to care, Sydney. Is that too much to ask?" I opened my mouth and then realized the question was rhetorical. "I wanted him to look at me and know what he'd done and say he was sorry."

"So you established yourself here and kept waiting for him to recognize you?" It was pathetic, in a way. "And kidnapping is your idea of a conversational opportunity?" Silly question: it was essentially what he'd just done with me. Kai was nothing if not consistent.

"You know how any times I tried to connect with him? I've been here *four years*, Sydney. And yeah, I like the town. And yeah, I like the work. But I kept trying to see him, trying to talk with him, and he'd never give me the time of day." He took a deep breath. "So I thought, fine. I'll make him listen. I'll even ransom him, get some money to travel, in case he didn't want to—in case things didn't work out between us."

"Wait. You thought you could kidnap Vincent and hold him for ransom and then let him go and everything would be okay? That he'd maybe have you come live with him or something?" That sounded breathtakingly stupid to me. Then again, we only know about the stupid crimes, and there are certainly enough of those around.

"I didn't think that far," admitted Kai, which was the most sensible thing I'd heard out of him yet. You could almost feel sorry for the guy.

Almost.

Evil isn't always brilliant. Evil can be pretty stupid, too. Kai was no Dr. No.

"So what went wrong?" I asked.

Kai was staring straight ahead through the windshield. "He didn't know," he said, slowly, and I could feel, physically feel, the pain coming off him in waves. "Four years I spent trying to have him notice me. Trying to get close to him. He didn't notice me, and it turns out there was a reason for that. After all this time, imagine stupid me, stupid Kai, thinking he just didn't care, thinking he'd abandoned us, and after all that, after everything, it turned out he *didn't know*. My mother left him when she was pregnant. She never told him she was. He never knew he had a kid. All these years, telling me what a bastard my father was, stoking the anger. Christmas, saying, 'he doesn't care about you, he doesn't care about you,' like it was a song, like it was a refrain, and now I see she was glad. Smiling all the time. 'No presents from him again this year.' She hated my father, and it turned out she hated me, too. And she took it all out on me." He brushed a tear off his cheek. "She never beat me, did I tell you that? I wasn't what you'd call an abused kid. Never lifted a hand to me. Oh, her brothers did, sure. My uncles. Trying to make me the man in the family. Teaching me discipline. Said my father didn't come around because I was weak. Because I wasn't man enough. Whole family said that, every chance they got. I was gonna prove them wrong. I was gonna prove them all wrong."

"By getting your father to acknowledge you." I paused. "Your mother is Clara Benevides." It was the only thing that fit.

Kai just nodded.

"So you kidnapped him."

He wiped more tears away, sniffed more back. "I gave him enough chances, Sydney, don't you see?" His voice turning eager. "I did everything. He went out on the first watch of the season every year, it was his thing, and I made sure I was signed on for that trip. Every spring. I'd bump into him on person. He'd stand up with the captain in the wheelhouse with his fucking glass of champagne, toasting himself, and I made sure I was in his line of sight. Sometimes I'd say something to him. Stop in at the Governor Bradford, stop over at Café Maria when he was hanging out with his cronies, say hello, remind him who I was. I gave him every chance in the world. All he had to do was recognize me. Remember he had a kid. Remember he had a son. And when he didn't…"

"When he didn't, you finally made damned sure he would."

He nodded. "Grabbed him when he was drunk, reeling. Told him I had some special Beirão—that's a Portuguese liqueur, very special, nice for settling your stomach at the end of the day. He said he didn't know I was Portuguese. Said we'd make a night of it."

"Where'd you take him?"

"Yacht in the harbor. The *Sassy Lady*? You ever see it?"

"Maybe."

"Not mine, belongs to the brother of a guy on the board at the Center. He's somewhere in Canada, left the boat there for the summer. They pay me to look after it for him."

So I'd been right. It was cold comfort, now. "So he went along."

"He couldn't get there fast enough. Climbed on board under his own steam. We sat drinking for a couple hours. I told him to spend the night, sleep it off. He was only too happy. I chained him up while he was asleep."

"When did you find out?"

"That he didn't know? The next day. I'd planned it for so long. It was perfect. He was hung over and easy to deal with. I let him use the head. That's the toilet. Even gave him something to eat, cooked him breakfast, eggs and potatoes. He kept asking why, why, why,

why... I just wanted to see his face when he realized. Realized he'd done this to himself. That he'd failed me. That I was giving him another chance at a real life, a real son. And find out why he'd hated my mother so much that he'd put her through everything. Both of us. That he'd put both of us through all that." He swallowed, hard. "He just kept staring at me. You can't fake that kind of surprise. I knew it before he even opened his mouth. I knew what he was going to say. I knew it was all down to my mother, that he didn't know, that she hadn't told him." He finally looked at me. "And you know what, Sydney? He was *happy*. Happy to know he had a kid. Kept saying, 'if I'd only known, if I'd only known'... He was going to change all that. Acknowledge me. It was all going to be different, he said."

"You believed him?"

"Why wouldn't I?" He looked genuinely surprised. There was something, I realized, oddly immature about Kai, zeroing in on a simple solution to a complex problem, the little boy who'd only ever wanted his father there at Christmas and thought he could make everything all right. It didn't occur to him Vincent might not have believed him—or that Vincent might hand him over to law enforcement as soon as he could. He wanted it to be so, and so it was—for him. "I took a picture of him with the newspaper to send to the police. I thought it would buy us a little time, you know, if I did the ransom-demand thing. He said I didn't need a ransom, he had enough money to take care of me, but then when he saw I meant to do it anyway, he said not to ask Marie for the money, said to ask Glenn Rogers at the Race Point Inn. Said Glenn owed him one."

"He saved Glenn's life," I said.

He nodded. "See? He was a good guy. He wouldn't ever have abandoned me."

I took a deep breath. I had no idea why Kai was telling me all this, but I didn't see how keeping him talking was a bad thing. Until I could figure out something more constructive to do, that was. "So what went wrong?" I asked.

"He got loose," said Kai. "I wasn't on board. I don't know how he did it. Maybe I was sloppy. Maybe I thought he'd stay there even without being restrained." Yep: not one of the great criminal minds of the century. Oddly, though, that stupidity made Kai more and not less dangerous. "I was motoring out to the yacht when it happened, and I could see him moving around. Scared the hell out of me. I scrambled on and went after him. I just meant to knock him out. You know, so I could tie him up again. Better. I had the skillet from breakfast, the breakfast I'd cooked him, and I hit him with it. And then he was dead."

I could picture Kai standing there, staring in disbelief, the pan slipping from his hand to the deck. The little boy who had broken his new present on Christmas morning.

He was brisk now. "Anyway, I dumped him over and cleaned the place up. No money. No father." There was something new in his voice: Kai feeling sorry for himself.

"It must have been hard to keep it together after that," I said.

He let out his breath in a gusty sigh. "My mother—I'd always known she was hard. You know? Coming up in New Bedford, on the docks, life wasn't easy. And she held grudges, man did she hold grudges. She never forgave my dad for divorcing her. So when I told her what happened—when I told her about him—she didn't waste any time getting here. I didn't ask her to, I would've been fine her staying there in New Bedford forever, never seeing her again, but no, she just had to come. She just had to gloat. She said it was poetic justice, can you believe that? Kill your father. Oedipus, wasn't it?"

"But you didn't sleep with your mother."

"No," he said. "I killed her." He didn't say anything for a moment, drumming his thumbs on the steering wheel. "She should have told

me. All that time, she let me believe he didn't
care. She hated him, she hated herself, she
hated me. She was all about hate. I could have
had a dad all those years, and she took him
away from me. She made me hate him, too.
She should have told him, and she should have
told me. And she didn't. Maybe she even
hoped I'd kill him. Well, she got her wish. And
left me with nothing—nothing! No father. No
mother, because now, how could I ever stand
the sight of her again? She'd ruined my life."
He took a breath. "So I took her out for a spin.
One of the Center's boats. Said I had to talk
to her alone. She was gloating, I'm telling you.
Saying now the Dolphin Fleet was ours. Said
it was all working out just right. Telling me
killing my dad was the best thing I'd ever
done, telling me she was finally proud of me,
after all these years." He shook his head. "She
said I was finally a man. You have to see, I
couldn't let that happen. Couldn't let her
dance on his grave. Not after what she'd done
to us."

"I can see how you'd feel that way," I said
cautiously.

"I cut her," Kai said. "I had a knife, I'd
brought cheese, her favorite, said it was a pic-
nic. I had the app out—Sharktivity, you know?
I wanted to take her out farther, but don't you
know, there one was, right off Long Point,

right in front of us almost, and it felt like a message. A message from my dad. So I cut her, lots of blood, and pushed her over. And you know what I said to her?"

"What?"

"*This* is what poetic justice looks like. That's what I said."

There was a long silence. I couldn't think of anything to say. Kai's story was over, and now we were approaching the main event of the afternoon: what to do about Sydney.

I wasn't in any hurry for that to happen.

The air in the closed car was stifling. "Can you turn the air conditioning back on?" I asked. "I don't know about you, but I can't breathe."

He looked shocked. "Do you know how bad it is for the environment, a car idling? Don't tell me you ever do that?"

This was surreal. Kai, protector of marine mammals and the environment, killing both his parents. "Well, I'm going to pass out in another minute," I promised him.

"Oh, for God's sake." He turned the ignition key so he could lower the windows. As soon as it was on, I reached behind me, found the lock, and had the door open in a second.

I didn't waste any time. I probably should have run toward the main buildings, the old barracks, where there were probably some people, artists in studios, maybe even Payomet staff prepping for the evening's concert, doing sound checks. That would have been the smart thing to do.

But even closer to the parking area was the path to the old base neighborhoods. And that's where I ran.

***

Kai wasn't the only one who didn't have a plan. I wasn't thinking, just running blindly. Behind me I hear the slam of the car door and Kai's voice. "Sydney! Don't be stupid! I just want to talk!"

Yeah, well, every time this guy had wanted to talk with someone, that someone ended up dead in the water. As in, really dead. I wasn't taking any chances. The long grasses and nettles scratched my bare legs—what a day to have worn a dress instead of far more sensible jeans! —but I just ran. Trying to remember which houses were accessible.

Past the abandoned playground, running as hard as I could remember ever running before, gasping... *breathe, Riley, just breathe...* and then, finally, there was a gaping doorframe. I ran in, trying to make no noise, back through the tiny living-room and into the corridor, the bathroom, round a corner and standing right beside the toilet bowl, my back against the partition for the bathtub, invisible from the door.

Or so I hoped.

And trying to tame my breathing; the heat and the running and all I wanted to do was double over, gasp for air, and I couldn't. Somewhere I read that once you've killed, it becomes easier, some sort of Rubicon has been crossed...

I'd also read rabbits will lose their nerve and bolt at the last minute. I didn't intend to do that.

Kai wasn't far behind me. "Sydney! Come on, you're making everything worse. Please don't do this." *I'm the one making things worse?* "Sydney. I'm not going to hurt you. Really."

He was coming closer. What if he popped in through the window, the small bathroom window I was facing? What if he slipped into the house, into the bathroom, without me seeing? I couldn't see the door. He could be in the house right now. He could be coming closer...

My nerve broke, and I took off out of that house like the favorite in the hundred-meter dash.

He saw me, of course. He was younger than me, stronger than me, healthier than me. I ran back farther and farther, darting behind one small house and then another, with Kai if anything sounding amused. "Sydney, you're being ridiculous. This isn't going to work. You know I'll catch you."

"And do what?" I yelled. I shouldn't be shouting. I needed to keep my breath for running, though right now it felt like my lungs were trying to push their way through my chest, like the alien in the Ridley Scott movies.

That wasn't all. Maybe all the people who used to live here had left of their own accord—I was willing the believe that—but I could feel them around me, the women in their pedal pushers, the children running amuck, yelling and laughing, the smell of brownies baking in the tiny ovens wafting over... *You're losing it, Riley.* I grabbed a tree and tried to figure out where I was. I'd run clear of the neighborhood, running from Kai, running from the ghosts of families long gone. No more houses, no more abandoned neighborhoods, just a tangle of short, stunted trees and bracken, and a roaring from somewhere close.

It was the ocean. I was close to the clifftop, someplace I decided I most emphatically did not want to be. Choosing between Kai and the cliff. Maybe he wouldn't even allow me the choice. *Breathe, just breathe...* If I cut off to the left, running parallel to the shoreline, then maybe I could make my way into the main base buildings. Or over toward the FAA radar installation. That might be the safest: surely they had cameras there, people on guard? Beyond that, just more forest, and then the Jenny Lind tower. Oh, there's a great idea, Sydney. No one would find me there. Kai could just let my body rot…

"Sydney! Where are you?"

My heart was hammering; if my lungs didn't burst out through my chest, my heart surely would. *If I survive, I swear I'll start exercising. I swear I'll join a gym. Really I will. Really. This time I mean it.*

The hammering was getting louder and louder, ridiculously so, and I burst out from the trees just in time to see the helicopter landing, its rotors beating the air in time to my heartbeats, in time to my gasps.

Ali was out of it before it even touched down. Instead of coming to save me, however, he was taking off after Kai, who apparently decided I wasn't worth pursuing anymore. More slowly, Mirela slid out and came running over to me. "Sunshine! Are you all right?"

"Tell me that isn't Guy's helicopter," I managed to gasp.

"Of course it is." She looked puzzled.

"Do I have to go in it?"

"Of course you do."

If there's one form of transportation I like even less than being on a boat with miles and miles of ocean under me, it's in a fishbowl with a lot less than a mile of air below.

It was shaping up to be just that kind of summer.

17

W ell, no one told me I was supposed to be worried, so I wasn't."

"That's fine, Ma."

"I mean, I would have worried if I'd known. But your father and I were taking a nap."

"I know, Ma."

"We had no idea you weren't somewhere around here, doing whatever it is you do."

"Don't worry, Ma."

We'd missed dinner. By the time the Truro police, and the Provincetown police, and the National Seashore Park rangers, and the FBI, and someone from the FAA—I kid you not— got through with us, there was no chance to make it to the restaurant, even if I'd felt up to fine dining.

Which I didn't.

We ended up in Glenn's office with a stack of takeout boxes from the Provincetown House of Pizza and bottles of Bass and Newcastle Brown Ale that Guy had brought along from somewhere. Probably from wherever the helicopter had come from; he had more tricks up his sleeve than Mary Poppins had in her carpetbag. I'd given up being surprised by anything he did. My parents, sitting together on the couch, looking bemused. Guy. Mirela. Even Julie had joined the charmed circle. "I'm off-duty," she said, helping herself to a beer. "Paperwork tomorrow."

My mother was asking the questions I'd already asked, and had answered, back in North Truro. "How did they know where to find you?"

"Luther," I said. "He was out doing some repairs to the Payomet performance tent." Just a few yards from us. I didn't see him; I was otherwise occupied." Luther, handyman extraordinaire, had called Glenn. Who called Ali, and then followed it up with a call to Mirela, just in case. And Mirela was with Guy.

In more ways, I gathered, than one.

And finally there was Ali, sitting next to me and holding my hand with a fierceness I didn't know if I should find flattering or scary.

Kai wasn't here; Kai wasn't ever going to be here again. When he saw the helicopter, when Ali started after him, he just ran. In the direction I'd been avoiding. It was unclear whether he meant to go off the cliff or not, but the rangers found his body at the bottom.

"So who owns the Dolphin Fleet now?" I asked. Julie laughed. "It'll take years to sort it out," she guessed.

"I don't think he wanted to own it," I said. "I think he just was reacting. He didn't think things through."

Ali said, "I see a lot of that in my business. Most criminals are people who can't reason from a to b. They can't reason, they don't think things through." He still hadn't let go of my hand.

"Sydney, I still think you should see a doctor."

"I'm fine, Ma."

"Aren't you friends with some doctor in town? Would it be that difficult for you to give them a call?"

"I don't need to see Thea, Ma. I'm fine."

"Well, if you're sure… I just don't understand any of this, I have to say. And he seemed like such a nice young man!"

"He was, Ma." Well, except for the murdering people part.

I was feeling incredibly sad. I'd been looking for grand gestures and nefarious plots, and all there really was in the end was this sad little boy who didn't know what to do with his anger. It was sordid more than exciting. They'd never be able to feature Kai in any mystery novel; he wasn't evil, not really. Just pathetic.

The beer was doing its work, and I was feeling drowsy. Julie left first, then Guy. Mirela stayed a little while. "I am not saying yes, and I am not saying no," she told me. "I am saying there is a lot he will have to do for me to make a decision."

I had a feeling Guy was willing to wait. I thought his chances were good; she hugged me on her way out, definitely out of character for Mirela.

Ali had finally let go of my hand and I had hopes circulation might be restored within an hour or two.

He cleared his throat. "I—um—do have some news," he said. "No, not about all this—" a gesture that encompassed the pizza boxes, beer bottles, and other assorted detritus in the room— "it's about Alexandra."

The sudden stillness in the air was almost stifling.

My mother reached over blindly for my father's hand; she hadn't taken her eyes off Ali.

He finally realized she wasn't going to say anything, so he cleared his throat again. "We've traced her after she left Boston," he said. "She was taken to New Jersey, along with several other—girls. Young women."

"You were right all along," I breathed. "She was trafficked."

The shimmer had started up again. When I looked straight at Glenn's desk, there was nothing there; if I turned my head away, she was sitting on it, her legs crossed, one foot moving lazily up and down. All made of light.

"Yes," said Ali, nodding.

My father said. "What—where did she—did they make her—" He couldn't finish the question.

"I think she was bound for the sex trade, yes," Ali said, taking on my father's meaning if not his actual words. "But she wasn't going to let that happen. She organized an escape, her and three of the other girls. She was—the leader. She'd gotten them out, gotten them somehow to an abandoned building slated for demolition, kept them there, hiding out. Giving them pep talks. Telling them it would be all right. She sent one of them, one of the other girls, to get the police. But—there was an accident. A stairway gave way—the building was crumbling around them. By the time the girl got back with the police, Alex was dead. It was just a stupid accident. But she saved those three girls."

My mother had made a sound like a whimper but didn't say anything.

"For what it's worth," said Ali, "she probably died immediately, so she didn't suffer. And she'd gotten herself and the other girls out. It's fair to say your daughter was a hero."

"Why didn't we know this at the time?" I asked.

"She wasn't identified," Ali said, shaking his head. "There just wasn't enough to go on. Oh, they took DNA, but there was nothing to match it to. They did a missing-person search, but..."

"Alex was never a missing person," I said, nodding.

"Right. And—well, there were a lot of girls like Alexandra in these places. Still are. They can't all be traced. But my colleagues spoke to the guy they arrested; he's doing life in a SuperMax prison somewhere in the Midwest. He's the one sent you the photo, Edward, before he got spooked and moved the girls out of Allston without waiting for the ransom. There'll be some red tape, and some convincing, but we may be able to locate where she was buried, if you'd like to..." He let the sentence hang.

"No," said my father and "yes," said my mother at the same time.

"You can think about it," said Ali.

I looked at Glenn's desk. The light was dissipating. I wanted to ask her to stay.

"The other thing," Ali said, a little diffidently, "is the girl. The one who went to the police, and came back with them to find the stairway collapsed? She's a high school principal now, married, has a couple of kids, lives right outside Boston. She's agreed to talk to you, if you want her to. To tell you about Alex, about what happened." He swallowed. "She credits Alex with saving her life," he said. "And her daughter's only sixteen, but she's just been accepted to Harvard and wants to go to medical school."

He swallowed again and then said the rest.

"Her name is Alexandra."

Author's Note

As usual, most of what I've written about in terms of background is true. The Avellars—Albert and his son Aaron—did indeed start the whale-watching enterprise out of Provincetown in 1975, and the whole east coast of the United States followed suit. The Dolphin Fleet was sold in a regular transaction, not to a family member, and has certainly not been part of any abduction or murder schemes.

It's still the best whale watch anywhere; when you visit, make sure to go out. (And if you're browsing in a used-book shop and see Sue Ogden's Whale Watchers Want to Know, by all means buy it. She used to work for the Dolphin Fleet "back in the day," and her book is a lot of fun.)

I've taken some liberties with the abandoned North Truro Air Force Station. Everything I describe here was absolutely true—once; I'll confess to spending many happy hours tramping around the old neighborhoods and taking photographs inside the abandoned houses. Too many people did the same, however, and the National Seashore put up fences; when those weren't enough to keep people out, they finally razed most if not all of the houses. I've written about what it was like some years ago, not how it is now. But Google it and you'll see; there are some fairly irresponsible videos on YouTube (search: "Truro abandoned air force base") which go a long way in explaining why the place was first fenced off and later parts of it deliberately destroyed. It is now receiving a second life as the Highland Center for the Arts, home in particular to the Payomet Performing Arts Center.

There is a real Codfather on whom I based my character. New Bedford is a tough town and he ran a tough organization. He's still in prison as I write this.

Human trafficking is an underreported ongoing cluster of crimes I guarantee is happening right now in whatever community you call home. If you're interested in learning about it, check online with the Polaris Project: since 2007, Polaris has operated the U.S. National Human Trafficking Hotline, which provides a variety of options for survivors of human trafficking to get connected to help and stay safe. Through a network of nearly 4,000 partner service providers and trusted law enforcement, trained hotline advocates take tips of suspected human trafficking from community members and help survivors build plans so they can safely leave their situations or get the help they need to rebuild their lives. You can help.

My character Ali Hakim works for ICE, the enforcement arm of the Department for Homeland Security. By virtue of its charter, HSI is mainly concerned with international trafficking. You can find out more about their efforts online by searching on "Blue Campaign."

Acknowledgments

My cup overfloweth with gratitude to and for Arthur Mahoney of Homeport Press, who I am fortunate enough to call my friend as well as my colleague. Sydney belongs to him as much as to me.

And again as always I thank all the beautiful people of Provincetown, who generously allow me to use so many of their own special selves in my books. Any errors in their portrayal are mine.

Thanks this time around to Anna Avellar, whose first husband and father-in-law created the Dolphin Fleet (and indeed the pastime of whale watching), and who kindly answered countless questions about it.

To those who contribute in so many different and important ways to the creation of a Sydney story: Colin Kegler, Amanda Robinson, Susan Blood, Pat Medina, Cathy Knipper, Chip Capelli, Robin Fredey, Ann Robinson, Michael Ponestowski, Freddy Biddle, Carem Bennett, Michelle Crone (whose wedding planning inspires Sydney, and who first suggested this series), Bob Allen, Julie and Katy

Blackburn, Lady Di, and Tony, Suzanne, and Albert Rodrigues. Thank you to my beautiful family, Anastasia, Jacob, and Sydnia Czarnecki; and to Sister Kathryn, for always inspiring me to do—and be—better.

Thanks to Deborah Karacozian, Nan Cinnater, and Clayton Nottleman for being my emissaries at the Provincetown Bookshop; to Jeff Peters and East End Books—as well as to Amy Raff and Brittany Taylor of the Provincetown Public Library—for fabulous book launch parties; and to Miladinka Milic for Sydney's amazing cover designs.

A special thank you to Carol and Barbara, to Julie K., and to Elisabeth in Canada, for being such super fans.

Thanks to Erin Delaney for editing, and to my wonderful First Readers: Kimberlee Sams, Corinne Diana, Margo Nash, Dianne Kopser, and A.C. Burch. Any mistakes that remain here are mine, not theirs.

My gratitude goes out to you all, to all of my beautiful seaside home, and to anyone I might have inadvertently left out—for sometimes I am a bear of very little brain.

No, not that kind of bear.

About the Author

Jeannette de Beauvoir writes mystery and historical fiction (and often books at the intersection of the two) that uncover dark secrets and hidden truths, while exploring a sense of connection to place.

A Book Sense Book-of-the-Year finalist, she's a member of the Authors Guild, the Mystery Writers of America, Sisters in Crime, and the National Writers Union.

Her delight is to find characters true to the spaces in which they live. She herself lives and writes in a cottage in Provincetown, on Cape Cod, Massachusetts, and loves the collection of people who assemble at a place like Land's End.

Find out more at jeannettedebeauvoir.com.

Did You Enjoy This Book?

If you did, please…

1) **share your opinion** on Goodreads and/or Amazon;

2) **visit my Amazon page** and check out some of my other books;

3) give the book a boost; **tell people about** it on Facebook and Twitter;

4) **subscribe to my newsletter** at **jeannettedebeauvoir.com** for book reviews, short stories, quizzes, free stuff, previews of upcoming work, and more;

5) ask your local bookseller **to stock** Sydney Riley books;

6) make them your **choice for your next book club** meeting (I'll even join you by Skype or Zoom if you'd like me to!);

7) **email me** at jeannettedebeauvoir@gmail.com;

8) and **watch for** the next Sydney Riley mystery from Homeport Press